Also by
ALI STANDISH

The Ethan I Was Before

August Isle

ALI STANDISH

HARPER

An Imprint of HarperCollinsPublishers

ISBN 978-0-06-243341-1

Typography by Joel Tippie
19 20 21 22 23   CG/LSCH   10 9 8 7 6 5 4 3 2 1

❖

First Edition

For Mom, who wrote me into her story

She was going to leave me again.

I could tell by the warm flush on her cheek, the way her eyes darted eagerly around the house as if she were already gone, already seeing things Dad and I couldn't.

Mom never looked that happy anymore unless she'd gotten her next assignment.

Reluctantly, I paused *Baking Battles* and trudged into the kitchen, where steam coiled up from the pizza Dad had just picked up. Hawaiian. My favorite.

As I sat down in my usual spot, Mom draped herself into the opposite chair and tugged a piece of pizza free from the box. Holding it in her right hand, she began to eat. Her left fingers drummed lightly against the table.

"So," Dad said. He dropped down into his seat, but his shoulders stayed stiff. "There's something we need to talk about, kiddo. Well, something Mom needs to tell you."

Dad always carried a sigh in his voice when he had bad news. Mom pinned on a smile. She looked like a doll, like something made just to be perfect.

I looked more like Dad.

"I'm going on a trip, Miranda," Mom said.

A knot rose in my throat. Without realizing it, I must have been holding on to the tiniest bit of hope that I was wrong.

"You've only been home a week," I protested.

"I know," she said. "But this is a really good assignment. Documenting the effects of climate change in Argentina. The photographer they had lined up canceled, and the magazine asked me to step in."

Mom worked for lots of newspapers and magazines, going wherever they sent her, taking pictures of elections and earthquakes, festivals and floods. She traveled a *lot*.

Sometimes it felt like she just came home to sleep off the jet lag for a few days before chasing her next assignment.

"The story's for *Witness*," she added. I could hear

the excitement in her voice, but I couldn't bear to see it glittering in her eyes, so I stared at my empty plate instead. *Witness* was a major magazine. If she did a good job, it would mean more commissions for more national magazines. More trips.

More time away from me.

"When do you leave?" I asked.

"A few days."

I looked up to see a glance pass between Mom and Dad. I wished I could reach up and snatch it from the air, unfold it, and read what was written inside, like a note passed from Kelsey Mays to Tiffany Rubald in the back of Mrs. Painswick's class.

"What?" I asked.

When Mom didn't answer, Dad ran his hand over his stubbly chin. "It's just that this assignment is going to be a little longer than most."

"Only a month," Mom added quickly. "I'll be back before you know it."

"A *month*?" I yelped. Mom's shoots usually didn't last more than a few days. "Can't we go with you?"

Mom's doll smile faded a little as she met my pleading gaze. Her eyes were a swirl of blue and gray, the color I've always imagined the wind would be if you could see it. The color of something you can never quite seem to catch.

"I'm sorry, kiddo," Dad said. "But I've got to be here

for the Anderson case. And this isn't the kind of shoot where a kid can tag along."

Dad was a lawyer, and he had this big case about to go to trial. So big he was planning to stay over most nights in Chicago, where it was being tried.

"Then what am I supposed to do?" I asked. "Stay with Gram and Gramps?"

I didn't exactly like the idea of spending the whole month with Dad's parents in Ohio. Gram made brussels sprouts every night, and Gramps blasted the Weather Channel on high volume all day long. But they were my only grandparents, and I was their only grandchild, so they did spoil me a lot. Maybe spending the summer there wouldn't be too bad.

Mom reached over and smoothed a stray strand behind my ear. I wished she would keep brushing her fingers through my hair, but her hand returned to her lap.

"Gram's still recovering from her hip surgery," she said. "They wish they could have you, but it just isn't a good time."

I felt my forehead wrinkling, my mind beginning to wander toward dark places. "You aren't sending me back to that camp, are you?"

Two summers ago, Mom and Dad had tried to send me to a summer camp—the kind with lakes and bugs and strangers.

I lasted approximately three and one-quarter days before finally convincing my counselor that if she didn't call my parents to come pick me up, I would hitchhike home.

"No," Mom said. "Much better. We're sending you to stay with Aunt Clare. Remember? She brought her daughter, Sameera, to stay with us when you were eight. You loved them."

"Aunt" Clare was not actually my aunt—I didn't have any real aunts, or uncles for that matter. She was Mom's best friend from childhood. She was really nice, I remembered, and Sameera was pretty cool, too, even though she had spent a lot of time showing off her gymnastics skills and also used all my toothpaste.

But that was four years ago, and Clare and Sameera lived all the way on August Isle, this little island off the coast of Florida.

"You're sending me to *Florida*?" I asked. "By myself? For a whole month?"

"I know it sounds like a long time," Dad said gently, "But before you know it—"

"—you'll be right back here in boring old Illinois," finished Mom.

Was that how Mom thought of where we lived? When you'd been to all the places she had, maybe it *was* a little boring. To me it was just home.

"It'll be fun, sweetie," she assured me.

Fun would have been spending the summer before eighth grade watching *Baking Battle* with Mom and cutting new recipes from magazines to add to my collection. I had actually thought this summer was going to be the one when we finally started trying some of them. Had hoped it so much I could almost taste them—the lavender-honey cupcakes with buttermilk frosting, the mile-high peach pie with cinnamon streusel topping, and the brown-sugar pound cake with bittersweet chocolate glaze. Except I would substitute milk chocolate for the bittersweet chocolate, because who needed more bitter anyway?

"I know it's unexpected, kiddo," Dad said, his jaw twitching as he glanced again at Mom. "But can we try to make the best of it?"

I looked up to see that the flush was gone from Mom's cheeks. She bit softly at her lip. I had stolen the happiness right off her face.

Guilt swam in my stomach like a fish in a tank, nibbling away. Mom had gotten a big break, and instead of being excited for her, I was ruining the moment. All because I wanted her to stay in boring old Illinois and watch TV with me.

I took a deep breath and dragged a little smile onto my face. "Okay," I said. "Sure. Why not?"

I could only think of about a thousand reasons.

Later that night, I sat with my back against my bed, listening to the familiar muffled sounds of Mom packing. She and Dad were having a conversation that might have been an argument, but their voices were too low for me to tell. On my lap sat Bluey, the one-eyed stuffed dolphin I had slept with every night since forever. In front of me was a box of postcards.

Sometimes I felt like Mom had a million secrets she kept from me.

I only had the postcards from August Isle.

Until Aunt Clare came to visit, the Isle had just been one of Mom's secrets. It was Sameera who told me that August Isle was where my mom had spent all her summers as a kid.

I didn't want Sameera to know that she knew more about my own mom than I did, so I waited until she and Aunt Clare left to ask Mom about the Isle.

"It's very . . . hot," she said.

"That's it?" I asked.

"It was a long time ago, Miranda," she said. "I was just a kid."

"Did Grandma and Grandpa Crawford live there, too?"

"They spent summers there, like me."

Mom didn't exactly keep my other grandparents a secret, but she didn't talk about them much either. All I knew was that my grandmother had been a painter, and my grandfather had been some kind of business-man who spent most of his time in New York City. But they had died before I was born, in a car crash near the town where Mom grew up in Connecticut.

"Could we go visit August Isle sometime?" I asked.

"There's a whole wide world out there full of places to visit, Miranda," Mom said.

Which I chose to take as a maybe.

But in all the trips Mom had taken, she'd never invited me on a single one. The only place we'd ever been together—besides to Gram and Gramps's—was Disneyland on my tenth birthday.

It was my best birthday ever.

Anyway, after Aunt Clare and Sameera left, I tried to ask Mom about August Isle a couple more times, but she always just said she didn't remember much about it.

I wasn't surprised. There were so many things Mom didn't want to talk about. Like why she became a photographer, or why she and Dad argued some nights when they thought I was asleep, or why I was an only child.

Or why I sometimes caught her looking at me like I was a stranger who had wandered into her house.

So after a while I stopped asking about August Isle, and I didn't think much more about why she wouldn't talk about it. Not until the day I came home from school to find a postcard from Aunt Clare in the mail. Mom was traveling then, so I got a magnet and put it up on the fridge for her to see when she got back.

A few days after she came home, I spotted the postcard in the trash, underneath a banana peel.

I glanced up at the refrigerator, still sprinkled with a collection of last year's Christmas cards.

It was October.

I fished the postcard from the trash, wiped off the banana goo, and took it to my room. I stared at the street lined with colorful brick buildings and rows of palm trees like it was one of those I-spy pictures, and if I looked long enough, I would find a reason for why

Mom had thrown it away. Or why she'd never told me about the Isle in the first place.

When I didn't, I got a tin box for the postcard and squirreled it away under my bed, next to the bulging binder of recipes I had never tried.

The next postcard arrived six months later and showed a Ferris wheel, looming bright over the ocean.

A few months after that one came my favorite, a card that showed a gigantic tree, light dappling through its lime-colored leaves.

I dug each one from the trash only days after it had arrived.

But none of the cards held any clues, and the messages Aunt Clare wrote were always short and cheerful.

Sending you our love from August Isle!
—the Grover family

So eventually I stopped looking for answers in them.

Instead I found myself gazing at their pictures and imagining me and Mom into them.

In my imagination, we would ride bikes on the beach and stroll down the cheery street, maybe wearing floppy straw hats. I would point up to the canary-colored building with the white trim that looked like a slab of yellow butter cake piped with royal icing. "What's that place?" I would ask, and Mom would look up and laugh and say, "Well, it's a funny story, actually. . . ."

Now I set all eight postcards in front of me and stared at them once more.

It wasn't that I didn't want to go to August Isle. It was the only place in the world I actually really wanted to visit.

I had just never imagined going by myself.

But maybe I was looking at it all wrong. Maybe I should think about my trip as a chance to investigate. Just because I hadn't learned anything about Mom from the pictures of the Isle didn't mean I wouldn't find any clues about her on the Isle itself.

Maybe I could at least find out more about why she didn't like to talk about it.

And maybe, just maybe, I would find something that would help me understand why everything had changed between us.

I tried to stretch out the next few days the way the contestants on *Baking Battle* stretched their pastry dough thin. But before I knew it, we were pulling into a parking spot at the airport.

Mom looked up from her phone, brushing her hair back from her face. "Are we here already?" she asked. "Gosh, that was quick."

"So remember, Mom's going to be pretty out of touch," Dad said.

"I don't know how much service we'll have up in the Andes," Mom added.

"But she's not leaving until tomorrow, so call us when you get to Florida. And call me anytime, okay?" Dad said, reaching back and squeezing my knee.

The three of us got out of the car and walked toward the airport. I carried my backpack while Dad took my rolly bag. Since she knew the airport like the back of her hand, Mom marched in front of us.

Inside, there were about a million people, including a lady with purple hair named Meg waiting to take me through security who I waved a shy hello to. Once we had watched my bag disappear behind the check-in desk, she stood to the side while I said goodbye to Mom and Dad.

"Well, this is it, kiddo," Dad said. I lunged forward and buried myself in his arms. If I burrowed deep enough, maybe I could still feel them around me when he left.

"Have fun," he whispered. "And remember to call, okay? I love you."

"I love you, too," I said. Then I turned to Mom.

She smiled at me as she unfolded her arms. For the first time all day, when she looked at me, I thought she actually saw me. For a second, I got a flash of the old Mom, the way things used to be. "Come here, sweetie."

Mom's grip wasn't as strong as Dad's. Her arms were light and slender, more like rays of sunlight you had to remember to feel. I wanted to let myself melt into them. "You're going to have a great time, okay?"

"Okay," I said. My heart was beating fast—too fast—and I clutched at her back when I felt her start to pull away.

She gave a brittle laugh. "Don't worry, Miranda," she said. "Everything's going to be all right. You believe me?"

"Yes, Mom," I lied.

"Good," she said, letting go. I forced myself to let go, too. "And Miranda?"

"Mmm?"

She wore a funny expression, and for a second I thought I might have seen a shadow of worry cross her face. Then she gave her head a little shake and it was gone. "Just—have a good time, okay? Be safe. I love you."

Then she and Dad were walking away, and my heart shattered into a million shards that flew into my chest and legs and fingers and throat and made them all throb with loneliness.

And even though Mom couldn't hear me, I whispered something to her, the same thing I always whispered when she left on a trip.

I imagined my words carrying through the airport and landing on her purse or sticking to her blouse, where they would cling like burrs until she finally looked down and noticed them.

And then she would hear me calling to her.

Please don't forget me.

Please come home.

In my earliest memories of Mom, she is reading me a story while I curl up on her lap. I can feel her fingers brushing lightly through my hair in the morning and her hand folding tightly around mine as she guides me across a busy crosswalk. I can remember how some nights, I woke up to find her crawling under my covers, wrapping her warm sunshine arms around me before we both fell back to sleep.

In those memories, Mom's love for me is fierce and sure.

But that was before she started traveling all the time. Before she started giving me funny looks, and before her love started to fade like the ink on Aunt Clare's postcards.

Sure, Mom still *said* she loved me. But I couldn't feel it the way I used to.

Sometimes I got flashes of the old love. Like when she looked at me that day in the airport. Or like when she took me to Disneyland.

It was a few weeks after the fourth-grade field trip to the aquarium that Mom was supposed to chaperone. I was scared to go on my own—all that water with just a flimsy layer of glass to keep it from crashing down around me—and she promised she would make it in time. But she got held up, and Dad came instead.

I think Dad must have had to miss an important meeting or something, because when Mom came home, they got into one of their hushed fights, and this one went on for a long time.

The next morning, Mom announced we were going to Disneyland, just the two of us, for my tenth birthday.

For three whole days, it was just Mom and me. She even turned her phone off, except to call Dad every night.

I had seen commercials for Disneyland, but I had no idea how big the roller coasters would be, and by the time we'd waited for an hour to get to the front of the line for one, I was too scared to go anymore. Mom didn't seem to mind, though. We did the smaller rides instead, and I held her hand tight.

The next day, my head felt all spinny, so we stayed in the hotel and had room service and watched funny movies and laughed until our stomachs hurt.

I thought it was the best trip ever. I thought Mom did, too. I started to hope that maybe things were going to go back to normal.

But when I reached for her hand as our plane back to Illinois took off, she winced. Once we were safely up in the air, she pulled it away and shook it like she had a writing cramp.

"Ouch," she said. "I think my poor fingers need a break."

A few days later, Mom flew to Alaska to take pictures of glaciers. And when she came back, she was more distant than ever.

On my plane to Florida, purple-haired Meg sat me down next to an old man with little red veins in his cheeks who took up the whole armrest.

I did not hold his hand.

When I got off a few hours later, another airline employee—this one a man named Joey—was waiting to take me to where Aunt Clare and Sameera were supposed to meet me. He didn't say very much, which was nice, because I never had a clue what to say when adults I didn't know tried to talk to me.

Then we got to the end of the terminal, and I held

my breath as I scanned the crowd for Aunt Clare and Sameera. I had only just realized that I had no idea what either of them looked like now. What if I couldn't find them?

But then my eyes fell on a slim girl in a cute spaghetti-strap dress who was holding a poster-board sign and jumping up and down. The sign said WELCOME, MIRANDA!!! in big glitter-glue letters. Next to the girl was a beaming blond woman.

Sameera dropped her sign and ran over. I stiffened as she threw her arms around me. "Miranda!" she cried. "I'm so happy you're here!"

"Thanks, Sameera," I managed. "Um, me too."

"Oh, you can call me Sammy," she said. "That's what everyone calls me now."

When she pulled away, I saw that she was shorter than me and that she'd gotten braces. It didn't look like she would have them much longer, though, because her teeth were shiny and straight beneath them. She had long black hair and bronze skin.

Next to her, I suddenly felt pale and shapeless in my wrinkled T-shirt.

If she went to our school, I thought, she would sit at the table with Kelsey Mays and Tiffany Rubald and the other girls who had stopped inviting me to their birthday parties around the fifth grade. Who giggled and whispered when I walked past in the cafeteria.

Yet there she was, dragging me through the crowd and grinning at me over her shoulder. Like I was the Queen of England or something.

"Mom! Mom! Look who I found!" she exclaimed as we reached Aunt Clare.

I suddenly wondered if this was just an act she was putting on for her mom. If as soon as we were alone together, the smile would slide right off her face. Sameera and I had gotten along well when she had come to visit, but would *Sammy* and I? She had come a long time ago, before the birthday invitations had stopped.

"Hi, Miranda," Aunt Clare said. "We're so happy to have you! I can't believe how big you've gotten." She wrapped me in a hug that smelled like pineapple and mint. It was a nice smell, but it just made me miss Mom's scent—red licorice and photo paper with just a dash of perfume.

Aunt Clare was pretty like her daughter, though they didn't look very similar until you noticed how their smiles were the exact same shape. She had sunglasses perched atop her wavy yellow hair, and freckles over her pale skin that made her look younger than Mom. She wore a sundress with turtles printed on it.

"Thanks for having me," I said. "I'm really, um, excited."

"Us too!" said Sammy, linking her arm through

mine and steering me toward the door. I muttered goodbye to Joey, who was asking Aunt Clare to sign something.

"Seriously," Sammy gushed. "You have no idea. Jessie decided to go to this summer camp, and Anita is visiting her grandparents in Poland. Those are my best friends, by the way. So I thought I was going to be all alone for the summer. Then your mom called my mom and said you were coming, and I was so psyched! Remember how much fun we had when I came to visit that once?"

The double doors opened and spat us out into the hot afternoon. The air felt like when you've just stepped out of the shower and all the steam is still trapped in the bathroom.

"Do you like Ferris wheels?" Sammy asked, swishing her hair over her shoulder. "Because there's this park by the ocean with a Ferris wheel and a little roller coaster and bumper cars."

Maybe she finally noticed that I hadn't said very much yet, because when we got to the crosswalk, she stopped and looked at me, her eyebrows crinkling together. "What's wrong?" she asked. "You don't like Ferris wheels?"

She seemed disappointed, even worried, and I realized that she wasn't acting. She really was just excited to see me.

{ 22 }

I decided right then that I liked Sammy, even if she was probably a popular girl, and even if she did use all my toothpaste that one time.

"No," I said, "I do. I remember seeing it on one of the postcards your mom sent."

"So," Aunt Clare said, catching up to us, "who's ready to head home? Amar and Jai are getting dinner ready for us there."

"Can I call my parents first?" I asked. "I told my dad I would let him know I got here."

"Of course! Why don't you call on our way to the minivan?"

She and Sammy walked a couple of paces ahead of me as I pulled out my phone. Dad answered on the first ring.

"Kiddo!" he said.

Warmth spread through my chest. "Hi, Dad."

"How was the plane?"

"It was fine," I said. "I'm with Aunt Clare and Sammy. It's really hot. And the air feels thick. Like soup."

"Well, that's Florida for you," he replied. "I'm glad you found them okay. Are you headed to August Isle now?"

"Yeah," I said. "Is Mom there?"

"Sorry, sweetheart," Dad said. "She went out to get a few things for her trip. Want to try her cell?"

"No," I said quickly. "It's okay. I'll just text her."

I didn't trust myself to talk to Mom without blurting out how much I already missed her, or confessing that every time she left, part of me worried that this time she might never come back.

"Anyway, we're at the car," I said, "so I gotta go."

"Thanks for calling. Have a fun first night, okay? Love you."

I waited for Dad to hang up, then slipped my phone back into my pocket.

"Ready?" Aunt Clare asked, opening the trunk of her minivan. Sammy lifted my rolly bag in before I could.

I nodded.

"Great," she said. "Then let's get our summer started, shall we?"

Sammy clapped her hands as I slid into the seat beside her. "Yes!" she said. "This is going to be the Best. Summer. Ever!"

She looked so confident that I could have almost convinced myself to believe her.

5

We drove down a highway that shot like an arrow between thick walls of pine groves and forests covered in blankets of some kind of ivy that Sammy called kudzu. Then we cut over onto a smaller road and wound through little towns that seemed to be crumbling into the ground in slow motion. On the side of the road, people were selling strawberries and peaches and boiled peanuts out of little wooden huts. When we came to a hut that was selling watermelons, we stopped, and Aunt Clare got out.

She came back hauling the biggest watermelon I had ever seen. "Voilà!" she said, straining to hoist it into the minivan. "Dessert!"

Pretty soon after that, we passed a sign pointing toward August Isle, and Sammy did a little cheer. "We're almost there!"

I felt my heart begin to beat faster as I craned my neck to get my first glimpse. Would I recognize the Isle from the postcards, or would it look different than I had imagined?

Sammy rolled down the window and motioned for me to do the same. A warm wind swept in like a fever as we started up an arched bridge. Below us stretched a wide ribbon of dark water and a harbor with speed-boats and sailboats lined up between wooden docks, bobbing like white ducks. I held my breath and clung to the door.

"Look!" Sammy said as we crested the bridge, pointing toward the windshield. "The ocean!"

I squinted against the sunlight. A town carved into neat blocks unfolded in front of us, a big hotel soaring on either end. Beyond everything else, I could just see a line of sparkling blue on the horizon.

It disappeared as we swooped down the other side of the bridge. We were almost across when I decided I couldn't hold my breath any longer and it burst from my mouth. My lips tasted like salt.

Sammy shot me a funny look. "Were you holding your breath?"

"Yeah. It's, um, just this thing I do."

"Why?" she asked, cocking her head.

I hesitated uncertainly. Before I could answer, Aunt Clare glanced at me in the rearview mirror and said, "To make a wish, right? You hold your breath over the bridge, you get to make a wish at the end. Your mom and I always used to do that."

"Exactly," I agreed, grateful to Aunt Clare for rescuing me. I made a mental note of what she had said about Mom, too. My first clue, even if it didn't seem like a very important one.

"How come you never told me I should hold my breath?" Sammy pouted.

"Because you might wish for something I don't want to come true," Aunt Clare said. "Like to be a grown-up already, or to have a flying pony in our backyard."

"Mo-om," Sammy grumbled, "I'm allergic to ponies, remember?"

"Which is why I can't allow you to wish for one," Aunt Clare replied. "See? I'm just looking out for you."

Sammy rolled her eyes, but I thought Aunt Clare was kind of funny.

As we cruised onto the Isle, I couldn't help but wonder what anyone who lived here would *need* to wish for. It was a town that looked like it was built just for people to take pictures of to put on postcards, and yet it was a hundred times better than my postcards had shown. They hadn't shown how blue the sky could be, floating along above us like a weightless river. They hadn't prepared me for how bright the flowers were that spilled from the window boxes of the buildings on Oak Street, or the way their iron balconies curled like hands cupped around whispered secrets.

I kept blinking, trying to take pictures in my mind of all the little details, to gather them up like a sweet bouquet. Beside me, Sammy was looking at something on her phone. The sun hovered just over her shoulder, perched like some bright tropical bird.

I leaned out the window, staring at the familiar brick storefronts. There was a blue café, a pink general store, and a green shop that sold dresses like the one Aunt Clare was wearing.

The canary-colored building—the one I had wondered about in the postcards—turned out to be a place called Sundae's Pharmacy & Ice Cream.

"Sundae's has the best ice cream in Florida," Sammy said, glancing up. "Maybe even the whole country. You'll see."

"Better look out the other side," Aunt Clare said, "or you'll miss the August Oak." She pronounced it "Aw-GUST."

She stopped at the only stoplight on Oak Street and pointed out the window. I gasped.

There was a little park there, reigned over by the most enormous tree I had ever seen. I remembered it from my favorite postcard, but I had no idea that it would be *that* huge.

The afternoon light made the leaves glow, and they fell into the shape of a giant golden bell.

"Wow," I breathed. "It's like its own forest."

"It's over four hundred years old," Sammy said. "The Isle's named for it, only people got lazy and started pronouncing it 'AU-gust' like the month."

"But why do they call it the Aw-GUST Oak?" I asked.

"'August' means something that's really impressive," Aunt Clare said. "Something that's earned people's respect."

"Oh," I said. I couldn't think of anything more august than this tree. "Can I take a picture?"

"Sure," said Aunt Clare, pulling the minivan over. I aimed my phone through the window, trying to capture how the light shone on the leaves. As we pulled away, I typed a text to Mom. "I'm here," I wrote. I hesitated for a second, then, deciding the picture was halfway decent, attached it under the text.

"Do you like taking pictures?" Sammy asked. "Your mom's a photographer, right?"

"Yeah," I said. "She is. I'm not that good at it, though."

Actually, last Christmas Mom had given me my own camera. It was one of those times when things suddenly felt good between us again. She woke me up early the next morning and took me driving around the countryside. It had snowed all night, and we pulled off onto a gravel road, then got out into this white forest. As we walked deeper in, Mom taught me how to set the focus and adjust the zoom. She talked about balance and perspective, and how to make the snow look white instead of gray.

Then we heard a twig snapping nearby, and we looked up to see a pair of deer, a fawn with its mother, each wearing a light coat of snow. They stared at us, unmoving. The winter sun shone through the trees behind them, turning them gold. Mom nudged me, and I lifted the camera.

I snapped my picture in a panic, forgetting everything Mom had just taught me. The sound of the shutter clicking sent the creatures bolting, but it didn't matter. Mom said the shot I had gotten was wonderful. She said I was a natural. She had it blown up and framed, and it hung now in our living room.

I never used my camera again after that. It had felt so good for Mom to be proud of me for something, and I was afraid if I tried again, she would realize that I had just gotten lucky with those deer. Then her pride would be gone, and the memory of that day would be spoiled forever.

Anyway, maybe deep down Mom knew it, too,

because she didn't offer to take me out again after that. When I packed for August Isle, I glanced at the camera before leaving it in my bottom drawer, where it had been ever since that day.

"My mom teaches piano," Sammy was saying, "but I gave up after I butchered my first recital."

"That was only because you never practiced," Aunt Clare said.

"I'm a journalist," Sammy continued, ignoring her mom. "Or at least I'm going to be. I want to be editor of the school paper next year. So I'm going to get the perfect scoop and have an article on it ready for back-to-school."

"What's the scoop?" I asked.

"I haven't found it yet," she said, her eyes narrowed in thought. "But I will. And you can help while you're here!"

"I don't really know how," I said, "but I can try."

"So what do *you* want to be when you grow up?"

"A baker," I said.

"Ooooh," Sammy breathed. "Like with your own bakery?"

"Yeah."

I guess I probably got the idea from all the baking shows I watched. I started getting into them right around the time that the kids at school started becoming really mean, and after my only real friend,

Caroline, moved away before sixth grade.

That's when I discovered that when you see a perfectly latticed apple pie, or a strawberry shortcake that's been layered just right, nothing else seems so terrible. Like there's no problem the right dessert can't solve.

"I didn't know you liked to bake," Aunt Clare said. "You'll have to make us something one night."

"Totally!" Sammy chimed. "You can teach Mom. She's worse at baking than I am at the piano."

"Thanks a lot," Aunt Clare said.

"Oh," I mumbled. "Um . . ."

I wished I had brought my binder of recipes with me. But even with them, I had never actually made anything myself, let alone taught someone else. Before I could come clean, though, Sammy was already chatting away again.

"I want to be like your mom," she said with a wistful sigh. "Traveling around the world, always chasing the next lead. Does she ever take you with her?"

"No," I said.

"Why not?"

"Because it wouldn't be appropriate for Beth to take her daughter to work with her," Aunt Clare said, saving me for a second time. "Just like it wouldn't be appropriate for your dad to take you into the operating room."

Sammy shrugged. "Still. I bet she's told you some awesome stories."

"Yeah," I replied faintly. "Totally."

Actually, I didn't like asking Mom about her work. It was too hard watching her face light up as she talked about all the distant places she'd been when she could have been with me.

Now we were driving down a row of houses with funny names like Pelican's Roost and Mermaid's Hideaway written on signs in front. The houses were painted bright colors, and some were even on stilts. They looked kind of like they had escaped from the circus, but in a pretty, not-scary kind of way.

Then, squished between Seahorse Chalet and the Crab Hole, there was a big house with no name. It was painted mint green and trimmed in white, with a turret at the top and a porch. It might have been nice, except that lots of the planks had been stripped bare of their paint, and some of the shutters were falling off their hinges. Tufts of long grass swallowed up the path that led from the street to the porch.

Nestled among the bright houses, this place stuck out like a rusted clasp on a string of perfect pearls.

"What's *that* house?" I asked, eager to get away from the subject of Mom.

"Oh, it's just an old place no one's taken care of," Aunt Clare said.

"Yeah," said Sammy, "because the old man who lived there *disappeared*."

"Sammy," Aunt Clare cautioned, flicking her eyes toward her daughter in the rearview mirror. "Don't tell tales."

"It's true!" Sammy protested. "Everyone knows it. Ten years ago, he—"

"*Sammy,*" Aunt Clare warned, "stop scaring our guest. Anyway, we're home now."

Sammy raised her eyebrows at me as we pulled into the driveway. "Later," she mouthed.

Sammy's house wasn't as big as some of the others on
the street, and it didn't have much of a lawn besides
a clump of palm trees on one side of the drive, each
frond like a tiny green firework. It was blue and sat
on brick stilts, with a big staircase that led up to the
porch and the front door.

"Wow," I said. "It's great."

"It's okay," Sammy said as she darted from her seat.
She reappeared by my side, slinging my backpack over
her shoulders as Aunt Clare tugged my rolly bag from
the back. I took it and dragged it awkwardly over the
shell-strewn driveway so she could carry the ginor-
mous watermelon.

"Just leave your bag there," Aunt Clare said when we got to the bottom of the staircase. "Jai will get it for you."

"My brother," Sammy said.

When Aunt Clare had come to visit us that one time, she'd only brought Sammy along. I knew Sammy had a brother, but I'd never met him or her dad.

I left my suitcase and followed Sammy and Aunt Clare up the stairs and inside, where I gulped in the cool air gratefully. It smelled like boy sweat and sunscreen and frying onions.

"We're home!" Sammy called. "Dad! Jai!"

I heard footsteps, and then a lanky man with tortoiseshell glasses appeared in the hallway. Sammy rushed over and wrapped her arms around him, and I felt a sharp pang of homesickness. Once Sammy had released him, he reached a hand out to me. "So nice to meet you, Miranda," he said. He had a faint Indian accent.

"Hi, Mr. Grover," I said, taking his hand.

"No, no," he said. "Mr. Grover was my father. You can just call me Uncle Amar. I'm making fajitas for dinner. I hope that's okay?"

"Mmmm," Aunt Clare said, stepping forward and kissing him on the cheek. "Sounds good."

The smell of the onions had made my stomach begin to growl, and I nodded eagerly. I could hear the sound of a guitar being played upstairs.

"Jai!" Aunt Clare called. "Come meet our guest! And get her bag, please!"

The guitar music stopped and a minute later a boy appeared on the stairs, maybe three or four years older than me and Sammy. He was tall, like his dad, and he had his dad's black hair, Sammy's hazel eyes, and Aunt Clare's pale skin.

"Hey," he said. "Jai."

"Hi," I said, staring at his band T-shirt because I didn't know where else to look.

"Yeah," Sammy said, following my gaze. "Jai got the music genes." She turned to him. "This is Miranda. Be nice to her."

"I'm always nice," Jai said. "Except to brats."

Sammy clicked her teeth. "I'm not a—"

"Go get Miranda's bag, please, Jai," Aunt Clare said. "Sammy, why don't you take her up and show her your room?"

"Come on," Sammy muttered, taking my hand and pulling me up the stairs. "You're sharing with me. I'm not bragging, but my room is totally awesome. You'll see why!"

She skipped down the hall and into her room. It was really neat—probably her mom made her clean it for me—and smelled less like sweat than the other parts of the house. She had a twin bed pushed up against the wall, a bedside table, a desk with a framed picture of her and two other girls, and a bureau covered in stickers. On the floor next to the bed, there was a mattress that had been made up with a pink blanket. She dropped my backpack on it.

"It's cool," I said.

"Yeah," she agreed, grinning. "But here's the really great part."

She bounded to a set of curtains and opened them to reveal a sliding glass door. Then she pushed it ajar and slipped out. I followed her onto a wooden side porch with a staircase going up.

The stairs led to a flat rooftop with a little railing going all around it, where there were a few lounge chairs and a table. From up here, you could see the whole town. Oak Street, and the top of the August Oak, the amusement park Sammy had told me about, with its familiar Ferris wheel, and the two big hotels. Beyond it all, the ocean stretched as far as I could see, unbroken except for a little island with a dark lighthouse poking out from a thick canopy of trees. I stared at the island, wondering why I hadn't seen *it* in any of the postcards. For some reason, it gave me a nervous feeling that made me shudder, so I turned my eyes back to the ocean.

The sun was starting to go down, casting a shimmering orange glow over the water. From way up here, it looked pretty and calm.

"I've never seen it before today," I said.

"What?" Sammy asked.

"The ocean."

Her eyes fluttered wide. "Seriously?" she said. "Never?"

"Well, I saw it once from a plane, when my mom and I went to California. But that doesn't really count."

Down on the beach, families were dragging umbrellas and blow-up toys back toward their houses. The tinkling song from one of the park rides drifted up to us on the wind.

"This must be a really cool place to live," I said.

"It's okay. Not a lot of people live here year round. In the summer, lots of stuff opens up for the tourists, but most of my friends usually leave. In the fall, they come back, but then the amusement park and other stuff shuts down."

"Sameera!" boomed a voice. "Dinner!"

Sammy rolled her eyes. "Dad still won't call me anything else."

"Why'd you change it?" I asked.

She shrugged. "Some kids made fun of it, and people would get it wrong sometimes, so I shortened it."

I frowned. I had thought Sammy was the kind of girl nobody would tease. "Why'd they make fun of it?" I asked.

"Look around tomorrow," she said, grimacing

slightly. "You won't see many other Indian kids on August Isle. At least I don't have to worry about my last name. 'Grover' is pretty easy to pronounce. People here usually don't think it sounds Indian, but it is."

I wrinkled my nose. The kids at my school made fun of me because I was shy and because I was good in math class and because I was bad in gym class and because I wasn't pretty like Kelsey and Tiffany. But nobody had ever been mean to me because of where my family came from. That was a different kind of mean, one I hadn't ever had to think about before.

"I'm sorry," I said. I felt bad for judging Sammy before actually getting to know her. "Kids really suck sometimes."

Sammy's face broke into a metallic smile. "Yeah. But not us."

"No," I said, grinning back. "Definitely not us."

"SUH-MEE-RAH!"

At dinner, I watched with interest as Sammy and Jai argued about whether or not one of Sammy's favorite singers lip-synced at all her concerts.

Even though they were fighting, I got the feeling they weren't *really* fighting. They were just fighting to talk. They were like one of those families on TV, where everyone is always rolling their eyes at everyone else, but really they'd do anything for each other.

I used to wish so bad that I had a little brother or sister to fight with like that. Someone who would follow me around and ask me annoying questions about everything. Someone who might think I was the greatest, coolest big sister ever.

But when I asked Mom, she told me she and Dad were done having kids, end of discussion.

So I invented an imaginary friend to keep me company instead. It was around the time I started school, I think. Right around when things started changing with Mom. I could still remember that his name was Batty, though I couldn't remember why anymore, because he was a boy, not a bat.

I did remember that we used to play together in the backyard, and once, we took a jar from the kitchen and went around catching fireflies. Batty said it looked like we had bottled up a bunch of stars, and then told me that he was going to be an astronaut when he grew up.

After that, we played astronauts and aliens a lot, and one day, I looked up from our game to see Mom standing in the doorway, staring at me like I really *was* an alien. It was the first time I had ever seen her look at me that way, and I knew instantly that I had done something wrong, and that I never wanted her to stare at me like that again.

"Who are you talking to, Miranda?" she asked.

"Batty," I said. "My invisible friend. He's going to be an astronaut."

"Oh," she said. Her frown tightened. "Well, maybe you should say goodbye to Batty. Then how about tomorrow I make a playdate for you with some kids at school? It would be nice for you to have some real friends to play with, huh?"

I stopped playing with Batty after that. I was lonelier than I had been before I made him up.

Sammy and Jai's argument ended when Aunt Clare said that neither of them knew what good music was and she would have to take them to hear a symphony sometime soon. Sammy and Jai groaned in unison.

When dinner was over, Sammy and I took our watermelon slices out on the porch and had a seed-spitting contest. To my surprise, I spat one all the way to the street and won.

"Oh my god," Sammy laughed. "That was crazy. Like a superpower or something!"

I giggled. "Yeah. The most useless superpower of all time!" Sweet juice was running down my cheek, and I lapped at it with my tongue.

Aunt Clare appeared in the doorway as we were starting our third slices. "You girls better finish up and get ready for bed," she said. "You have an early wakeup call in the morning."

"Why?" I asked.

"Oh, yeah!" Sammy said, doing a little dance. "We have a surprise for you!"

She looked at Aunt Clare, who nodded.

"We're taking sailing lessons!" Sammy exclaimed. "And we start tomorrow morning!"

The watermelon slice slipped from my hand.

Fear had always been a part of me, like my dimples, or my love for Hawaiian pizza.

I was scared of the dark, and of talking to strange adults, and of giving reports in class. I was afraid of baseballs, basketballs, footballs, and roller coasters. I was afraid that one day Mom would leave me for good.

I was also terrified of water.

When I started kindergarten, Mom insisted on taking me to swimming lessons.

"Please don't make me, Mommy!" I begged as she dragged me closer and closer to the rippling pool. "Please, I don't want to!"

If I got in the water, I knew, it would swallow me up. It would grip me with watery blue fingers and pull me down, down, down.

"We talked about this, Miranda," Mom said. Her voice was rigid. "You don't ever have to swim again after you learn, but you have to know *how*."

I went limp, and she picked me up and swung me over her hip, but her frame was as rigid as her voice. She walked me down the first few steps into the pool, where the instructor and the other kids stood, mouths gaping at me as I screamed into Mom's chest. "Please! Please! Please don't make me!"

But suddenly my feet were in the water, then my knees, and then my chest. Mom pulled me away from her like she would a crab pinching her toe, handing me a floating kickboard instead. I clung to it, splashing violently at everyone around me until I finally realized that as long as I held on to it, I wasn't going to sink.

Then I kicked back over to the stairs and ran out of the pool.

Mom and Dad both had to come back with me for private lessons, but eventually, I did learn to swim. And then I never set foot in the water again.

After my swimming lessons, I started having this dream.

In it, I'm wading in the water when suddenly something grabs me around the ankles and pulls me under.

I'm splashing and spluttering and one of my arms shoots out, reaching for help.

"MOMMY!" I yell.

But she doesn't come, and my legs and arms are getting tired. Too tired. Then, just as I'm about to sink beneath the surface, I wake up, gasping.

And that's how I woke up on my first morning in August Isle.

Sammy was staring at me from her own bed, her knees drawn up to her chest. "Are you okay?" she asked, eyes round.

"Yeah," I said, my breath coming fast. "Yeah, it was just a nightmare."

"I get those sometimes," she said. "I'm running downhill, and there's this big wheel of Swiss cheese chasing after me. I hate Swiss cheese."

I let out a shaky laugh.

"Come on," Sammy said, throwing off her covers. "It's time to get up anyway. Time to set sail!"

I gulped. The nightmare wasn't over. It was just beginning.

The only swimsuit I owned had been given to me for Christmas two years ago by Dad's great-aunt Lucille, who thought the pink frills on the hips would look "just ah-dorable" on me.

I had never worn it before, and when I put it on that

morning, it was to find that it was two sizes too small for me.

Mom probably hadn't remembered that it was so old.

She had finally texted me back after Sammy and I had gone to sleep.

August Oak! Beautiful pic. Miss you. Kisses.

I read her message at least ten times before Sammy and I went down to breakfast.

Downstairs, I told Aunt Clare that Mom had accidentally packed my "old" swimsuit, as if I had more than one. As if Mom had actually helped me pack.

"Oh, that's no problem," Aunt Clare said. "We can take you to buy one after your lesson. Better eat up and then get your sunscreen on! We have to leave in five minutes."

Once the three of us had piled into Aunt Clare's minivan, we drove past the street with the creepy abandoned house and by the August Oak—where tourists were already snapping pictures—and Sundae's. When we were almost back at the bridge, Aunt Clare turned into the harbor parking lot and stopped.

Farther down, there was a leaning wooden shack with a sign over it that said "Bait Shop" and then rows and rows of sailboats and speedboats and even the kind of huge boats I thought were probably called yachts.

By the parking lot was a little beach where a guy in a flamingo-pink swimsuit, sunglasses, and a backward baseball cap stood, waving to us.

"That's Jason," Sammy said. "My mom is in book club with his mom. That's how she heard he was doing lessons."

"See you in an hour and a half!" Aunt Clare called before pulling away. "Remember to put more sunscreen on if you get in the water!"

An hour and a half, I repeated to myself. It didn't sound so long. Just the length of two episodes of *Baking Battles*, which was practically no time at all.

Or the length of two gym classes, which was basically forever.

"Come on down, girls!" Jason called.

A few sailboats were tethered to nearby posts in the water. They seesawed back and forth, knocking into each other. A Jet Ski zoomed by, sending white swells rocking toward the boats.

Somehow, I could feel them rocking in my stomach, too. Was it possible to be seasick just from looking at the sea?

Sammy was already bounding toward the beach, and I forced myself to follow.

Jason had blond hair and coppery skin. When he took his sunglasses off to wipe the sweat from under his eyes, though, the skin there was snowy white. I guessed he spent a lot of time in the sun.

"Hey, Sammy," he said. Then he turned to me. "You must be Miranda. I'm Jason."

"Hi," I peeped.

"We're just waiting for one more," Jason said. "Ah, here he is now. I'll go get some life jackets."

I turned to see a boy ambling toward us.

Sammy hissed under her breath.

"What?" I asked. "You know him?"

"That's Caleb Dillworth," she said. "He goes to my school. He's *ugh*. In the third grade, he stuck his gum on my binder when I wasn't looking. Then *I* got in trouble for yelling at him."

"Gross," I said, wrinkling my nose.

"Hey, Sammy," Caleb said as he approached. He was my height with scruffy brown hair, plump pink cheeks, and a wide nose covered by a thick layer of freckles that looked like chocolate sprinkles.

"What are *you* doing here?" she asked.

"My mom's in the book club, too. She thought I should get out of the house," he muttered. "Who's this?"

I felt self-conscious when he looked at me, standing in my too-small swimsuit, the elastic digging into my blindingly white skin under the pink frills. I hoped he couldn't tell that he was making me nervous, but boys like him usually could.

"She's my friend, is who," Sammy said. "So just mind your own business."

"Let's get started," Jason called, hailing us down to the water. "I thought today we'd take the keelboat out together."

He turned and pointed to the largest of the four sailboats, about the size of Aunt Clare's minivan. "I'll show you what it is you're learning to do. Then tomorrow, we'll start you on these guys." He gestured to the smaller boats. "We'll get into the parts of the boat, how to work the sail, all that good stuff. Cool?"

"Cool," Sammy and Caleb said.

My mouth pressed into a silent line.

Jason handed us each a life jacket. "Strap these on and hop in."

Sammy and Caleb buckled their life jackets and waded through the water to the boat, just a few feet from shore.

I watched, frozen in place. Beads of sweat rolled down my cheeks. I felt like a melting ice sculpture.

"What's wrong, Miranda?" Sammy called.

"She looks like she has to use the bathroom or something," Caleb said. "You can do that in the water, you know. Unless it's—"

"Shut *up*, Caleb!" Sammy demanded. "Miranda?"

"Everything cool?" Jason asked, walking toward me.

"Um," I said. "I don't—feel good."

By now, I knew, my cheeks would be strawberry patches.

"Do you want me to call your mom?" Jason asked.

"No," I said. "Don't call Sammy's mom. I'm okay. I just—"

I took a small step forward. As an experiment.

Then I imagined being trapped on that flimsy boat in the middle of the ocean, and I felt another swell, this time of terror.

"I can't," I whispered. "I can't get on that boat. Couldn't you just go without me?"

Jason blinked at me, then looked around. "Bill is up at his bait shop," he said. "I guess he could keep an eye on you. But wouldn't you rather come with us? I mean, you're just going to be stuck here otherwise, with not much to do. He'll probably make you rake the beach."

"It's okay," I said. Raking the leaves was one of my jobs at home. "I don't mind."

He shrugged. "Okay, Miranda," he said. "Your call."

My stomach dropped at the disappointment that clung to his voice. He hesitated, then lowered a hand to my shoulder and squeezed.

As he jogged to the top of the beach to tell Bait-Shop Bill I was staying, Sammy lifted her palms in a "what's up?" gesture. I shook my head.

When Jason came back, he was holding a rake.

It felt like Sammy and the others were gone a lot longer than an hour and a half. When I was done raking the beach, I had nothing to do but stare out at the water I was too scared to cross. The sun was beating down, flashing diamonds across the blue harbor, making me squint and wish I had some sunglasses.

While I waited, a big sailboat drifted into the other side of the harbor. The word "Albatross" was painted on its side.

"Look what the cat done dragged in," I heard Bait-Shop Bill drawl.

"Is that what I think it is?" another man asked.

But just what it was—besides a big boat—I didn't

find out, because the two of them walked off to get a better look.

Finally a speck on the horizon turned into a blob, which turned into Jason's smaller sailboat. I waved as they skimmed closer and Jason lowered the sails. As soon as they were near enough to the beach, Sammy jumped out and ran toward me.

I was worried she would be mad at me for making her go alone with Caleb. But her eyes were full of concern as she skidded to a stop in the sand.

"Are you okay?" she asked.

"I'm sorry I didn't come," I said.

She shook some water from her hair. "It's fine. I was worried about you. So what happened?"

I considered making something up. Cramps, maybe, or a headache. But what excuse would I give the next day? I decided I was better off with the truth.

"I don't like water," I said. "Actually, I'm afraid of it. Like, really afraid."

Sammy pulled me into a wet, salty hug. "You should have said something earlier," she said. "Oh, wait—is that why you were so nervous driving over the bridge?"

"Yeah."

"We don't have to do these lessons," she said.

"No," I replied firmly. "Your mom probably already paid for them. I'll just—figure something out."

But what exactly that something was, I had no idea.

"Then I'll help you," Sammy said. "We'll do it together."

I smiled a wobbly smile at her.

Jason had made his way up from the beach and was leaning against the open window of Aunt Clare's minivan, which must have just pulled back into the parking lot. Caleb sauntered over, distracting me from trying to hear what Jason was saying. "Sammy didn't tell me you were royalty," he said.

"Huh?"

"Miranda the Sand Queen. Has a nice ring to it, right?"

"Leave her alone, Caleb," Sammy said, taking my arm. My cheeks burned as we started toward the parking lot.

"Later, Sand Queen!" Caleb called, staring at me as I turned away.

When we reached the minivan, Jason shot me a sympathetic look. "Hey, Miranda," he said. "Tomorrow's another day, huh?"

"Are you all right, Miranda?" Aunt Clare asked as we pulled away. She kept glancing at me in the rearview mirror, her eyes full of concern.

"She's not sick," Sammy said. "She doesn't like water."

Aunt Clare made a clicking noise. "I should have asked you before I signed you up for these lessons," she said, the lines around her mouth deepening. "It was a last-minute thing, but I should have—"

"No," I protested. Seeing how upset she looked was making me feel worse than I already did. "Honestly, it was really nice of you. And I have to get over my fear sometime, right?"

Actually, until the night before, I had planned to just never face it.

"Well, if you're sure," she said, biting her lip.

"I am," I said.

But I didn't think I had ever been less sure of anything in my life.

After I'd sort of survived my first sailing lesson, the day started to look much brighter.

Once we'd had lunch, Aunt Clare left for the music school on the mainland where she gave piano lessons, which Sammy said she did most afternoons. Sammy and I walked to a shop called the Two-Legged Flamingo. ("Don't all flamingos have two legs?" I asked. Sammy furrowed her brow, then laughed. "You're right!" she replied. "I never thought about it!") There I picked out a pair of sunglasses and a bathing suit that actually fit me and was neither pink nor frilly. Then we went next door to Sundae's for ice cream.

Inside was a regular drugstore. But along one wall, there was also an old-fashioned counter with swivel stools. Behind the counter, buckets of ice cream in every color shimmered in a glass case. Looking closer, I saw they came in strange flavors like cantaloupe and caramel apple.

We asked for samples of pretty much every flavor from the guy behind the counter before settling on our choices. Piña colada for me, and strawberry macaroon for Sammy. Then we took our cones and walked across the street to the August Oak, where we found an empty bench. Sitting there in the shade, I felt my shoulders relax for the first time all day.

"So what ideas do you have for your story?" I asked. "The one for your school paper?"

"I'm not sure. The only idea I had so far was sea turtles."

"Sea turtles?"

"Yeah. They're my favorite animal. The moms make their nests on the dunes around here in the summer. They lay all these eggs, and the sand around the nest gets roped off so no one steps on them. And then those babies will come back to the exact same place when it's time for them to lay *their* eggs. How cool is that? Almost like magic."

"It sounds like a good story."

"Yeah, but not a scoop. What's my angle? I need something with . . . an *edge*. I bet your mom would have some good advice."

"Yeah," I mumbled. "Probably."

I gazed up at the light trickling down through the leaves of the August Oak. Its branches were hung with clumps of wiry, brown stuff that Sammy said was called Spanish moss. The light made it glow. It reminded me of that old fairy tale Mom used to read me, the one with the princess who weaves straw into gold. I wondered if Mom had ever sat on the exact same bench and thought the exact same thing.

Then, when purple clouds blew the golden light away, we ran for home, scrambling up the steps just as thunder shook the house and rain began to pour. We squished into the hammock on the porch.

It was cozy and dry there, creaking back and forth, and after a while, Aunt Clare came home and asked if we wanted any lemonade.

I was still thinking about Mom, though, and about how I had planned to investigate her past while I was here. So far, all I had learned was that she held her breath going over bridges.

"Hey, Aunt Clare?"

She stopped in the doorway. "Mmm?"

"I was wondering . . . what was my mom like when she was a kid?"

A smile sailed across her face, like just the memory of Mom was enough to light her up from the inside. "How about I show you?" she said. "I actually pulled some old photos out earlier. I thought you might like to see."

Inside, Aunt Clare poured us each a glass of lemonade and led us into the living room. She handed me a stack of pictures. "Thanks," I said, taking them eagerly and sitting down on the couch.

The first one was of Mom and Aunt Clare standing on the beach and making funny faces into the camera. They looked like they were about the same age as Sammy and me.

"Wow," Sammy said. "You look so much like your mom."

I frowned. In the picture, Mom's limbs were long like mine, but they were willowy instead of awkward. Her hair had streaks of blond where mine was stubbornly brown. And she was beaming. Not with the perfect-doll smile I recognized, but with a real, crooked, ear-to-ear grin.

"I don't really see it," I said, flipping to the next one.

In it, Mom was on the beach once more, this time holding a surfboard.

"My mom knew how to surf?" I asked. "She never told me that."

"Oh, yeah," Aunt Clare said. "She was pretty good, too."

In the next photo, Mom and Aunt Clare were a little older, standing on a boat and holding up an enormous silver fish. They were surrounded by other kids, all laughing and flashing thumbs up.

"Wow," I breathed. "You guys had a lot of friends."

"Tourists, mostly. Your mom was really good at making friends with them. That summer she convinced a huge group of us to go deep-sea fishing. It was a really fun day."

The photos had started to make me feel oddly dizzy. I wasn't sure what I had expected to find in them, but they just made me more confused than ever. Why hadn't Mom told me about the surfing and the deep-sea fishing and all her friends when I'd asked her about the Isle?

I kept flipping. There was a picture of Mom riding her bike down Oak Street, waving with both hands at the camera, and one of her and Aunt Clare wearing diving suits.

"You guys really were best friends, huh?" Sammy said. "You did everything together."

It wasn't hard to see why Mom would be best friends with Aunt Clare, if Clare had been anything like Sammy. Mom would have wanted to be friends with a girl like her—fun and brave and adventurous. A girl with *edge.*

It was my own fault for asking, but I suddenly wished I hadn't seen these pictures at all. They made me feel the same way I did when Mom talked about how much fun she'd had on one of her trips.

I fought back the tears springing into my eyes.

"She looks so—" I murmured. For a minute, I couldn't think of the word. Then it came to me. "Different," I finished.

She did look different, but that wasn't really the word I was thinking of.

Happy. The word I was looking for was "happy."

10

Later that night, when Sammy and I were back in her room watching Netflix, my phone lit up. I looked down at my screen and saw the word "Mom."

"Hello?" I answered, chest swelling.

"Hi, Miranda."

"Hi, Mom." I gestured toward the sliding door. Sammy gave me a thumbs-up as I stepped out onto the porch and into the sticky night air.

"How's August Isle?" Mom asked. "Is everything going okay?"

I could hear a voice in the background calling out boarding groups. She must be at the airport.

"It's great," I said, forcing as much cheer into my

voice as possible. "I really like it here. And Sammy and Aunt Clare are so cool."

There was a pause, and I could tell she was listening to the announcements at the same time we were talking. "That's wonderful, sweetie."

"Actually," I said uncertainly, "Aunt Clare was showing us some pictures of you guys when you were kids."

"Oh yeah?" Mom asked. "Nothing too embarrassing, I hope."

"No," I said. "You looked like you were having . . . fun."

"Well, Clare and I had some good times together," she said. "I'm sure you and Sammy will, too."

There was so much I wanted to ask. But I didn't. Maybe because I knew better than to think Mom would actually answer my questions.

Or maybe because, deep down, I was already afraid she would.

Instead I told her about spitting watermelon seeds and the strange flavors at Sundae's and Sammy's plan to find a big scoop to write about for her school paper. "My favorite thing here is the August Oak," I said. "Did you ever notice how when the light comes through the leaves—"

"So sorry, sweetie," she interrupted. "They're calling my boarding group now. It sounds like you're having such a great time, though. I'm glad."

I really didn't want to hang up, but I knew I didn't have a choice. "Okay," I said. "I hope your flight is safe. I love you."

"Me too," she replied. "It might be a while before I can call again, but I'll do my best, okay?"

"Okay," I said. "Bye."

I sat out on the porch for a few minutes after that, just thinking about those pictures and listening to the ocean.

When I heard voices, I turned around, thinking Sammy might have come out. But after a second, I realized the voices were wafting up from the porch below.

"I think we have to talk about what happened at the harbor today," Aunt Clare was saying.

My chest tightened.

Uncle Amar let out a long sigh. "I don't like it," he said. "Are we sure—"

He hesitated.

"What?"

"Well, are we sure this is the right place for Miranda?" he asked. "I mean, considering today's developments? Should we call Beth and tell her?"

My heart began to pound. *No, no, no,* it beat. If they called Mom and told her I couldn't stay here, then she would have to cancel her trip. *Witness* magazine would never hire her again. And whatever was broken between us might never be fixed.

"I don't think we should," Aunt Clare replied after a long minute. My heartbeat slowed. "She's probably on her way to Argentina right now. It's not like there's anything she can do from there."

"Whatever you want," Uncle Amar said. "I do think she's saddled us with quite a big burden here."

"I know," Aunt Clare murmured. "But can you blame her? Look, I don't want to upset her. Let's just keep an eye on things."

There was another long pause. Then, "Let's change the subject, okay?" Aunt Clare said. "How was that meeting this morning?"

I waited silently as Uncle Amar told Aunt Clare about meeting with his boss, not even daring to slap the mosquito I felt biting into my shoulder. Only when they'd gone inside again did I slip back into Sammy's room.

"Come watch this video!" Sammy said when I slid back through the door. "It's a cat that ice-skates!"

I curled up next to her and laughed at the right moments as she took me on a YouTube tour of her favorite videos. But the laughter was hollow, and I began to yawn obviously until Sammy started to yawn, too, and decided it was time for bed.

Then I lay in the dark for a long time, Aunt Clare and Uncle Amar's words circling around my head like bloodthirsty sharks.

I do think she's saddled us with quite a big burden here.

I knew what "burden" meant. It was one of our vocabulary words last year. It meant something you had to carry. Something heavy. Something you didn't want.

I know, but can you blame her?

My mind became a movie reel.

I saw the time Mom discovered me playing with Batty and said I needed to make real friends . . .

And the day she took me for my swimming lessons and I clawed at her shoulders . . .

The plane ride back from Disneyland when I held her hand so tight, it hurt . . .

The summer I made her pick me up from camp . . .

The night she told me about her trip to Argentina and I stole the smile from her face . . .

Then I saw Mom, grinning in all those pictures with Aunt Clare. So happy.

It's no wonder she travels so much, said a voice inside my head. *It's no wonder things have changed between you. You* are *a burden. She was much happier before you came along.*

A tight knot rose in my throat.

If she had a daughter like Sammy, the voice hissed, *maybe she still would be.*

11

The next morning, I woke up exhausted but determined. I had stayed awake a long time the night before, thinking. Until finally I came to a decision.

I would no longer be Miranda, Sand Queen, burden to everyone.

I would be Miranda, brave and bold, always ready for a new adventure. Then maybe, just maybe, by the time I returned home to Illinois, I would be the kind of daughter who could make Mom happy again.

And I would start by overcoming my fear of water.

There was just one problem. When we arrived on the sailing beach that morning, Jason was pulling the little sailboats up onto the sand.

"Why are you doing that?" Caleb asked.

"We're staying on the beach today," said Jason. "Before I can take you out on the water in your own boats, you've got to learn what you're supposed to be doing out there."

Caleb scowled. Disappointment flashed across Sammy's face for just a second.

I took a deep breath, buckling my hands into fists. "We don't have to stay on the beach just because of me," I said. "I want to go out."

One eyebrow lifted above the frame of his sunglasses as Jason considered me. "Good to know," he said, "but you have to learn the basics before I turn you out in the water. Now, go ahead and claim a boat. We'll start with learning the parts."

As I walked to my boat, I kicked up a spray of sand. But when I finally loosened my fists, my hands were trembling.

We spent the first part of the lesson repeating back the names of the sails (jib and mainsail), the poles (mast and boom), the ropes (halyards, boom vang, sheets), and edges of the boat (bow, stern, starboard, port). Then we moved on to learning how to tie different kinds of knots with names like old-timey dance moves (bowline, clove hitch, figure eight).

By the time we trudged up from the beach, everyone looked red and sweaty and bored. Aunt Clare was already waiting to pick us up. I said hello without looking at her. I hadn't been able to look her or Uncle Amar in the eye since last night.

She wasn't the only one in the parking lot. A few men trudged back and forth, carrying big wooden crates from one of the boats in the harbor to a truck parked outside the bait shop.

"Wonder what that's about," Sammy mused as she climbed into the minivan, her head turning to follow one of the men.

"Maybe we should ask," I offered. "It could be a lead. Something you could use for your story."

But Aunt Clare was already driving out of the parking lot. "Honestly, it's probably just old boating equipment someone's getting rid of," she said gently. "Besides, I thought you were doing a story on sea turtles. Why don't you take Miranda to the beach to see that nest today?"

Sammy gave a long sigh. "Oh-kay," she said, her voice flat. "I wish something *actually* interesting would happen in this town."

"Careful what you wish for," Aunt Clare muttered, her eyes flickering back to us in the mirror, then quickly flitting away again.

Later that morning, Sammy and I walked out to the beach. She took off her shoes and turned cartwheels across the sand while I watched. Sammy might have changed her name, but apparently she still loved gymnastics.

I followed her over to where Jai was working a lifeguarding shift. He sat at the top of a small white tower. A few girls in bikinis stood in the shade of his umbrella, looking up and laughing.

"Hey, Romeo! You're supposed to be keeping people safe," Sammy called as we walked past. "Not flirting with the tourists."

"Ignore her," he said, not bothering to look up from the girls. "She's just my kid sister."

Sammy stuck out her tongue. "You're so lucky you don't have a brother," she grumbled.

"I don't know," I replied, thinking of Batty. "Being an only child is lonely sometimes."

"Well, you're lucky you don't have *my* brother," she said, glaring at the girls as she unclipped a life jacket from Jai's lifeguard tower—one of those embarrassing bright orange ones—and handed it to me. Then her face brightened. "Come on. This is going to be fun!"

I followed her toward the water, my heartbeat growing louder with every step. When I looked back at Jai, he was still flirting.

"So he's not going to watch?" I asked.

"He'll keep an eye out," Sammy said. "He's just pretending not to, to make me mad."

We stopped when we reached a ribbon of shattered shells in the sand. Beyond it was the surf, roaring and foaming like a crazed animal. And I was about to walk into its jaws.

"Are you okay?" Sammy asked. "You look kind of pale."

"I'm kind of always pale," I said.

"True," Sammy replied, laughing. "Okay, let's take it one step at a time."

She took my hand and squeezed. We hopped over the shells. I gasped as a wave surged in and my ankles disappeared beneath it.

Swimming lessons in the pool were one thing. I could see straight to the bottom there. But this water was different. Darker.

"Do you ever worry?" I asked before I could stop myself. I flinched as another wave rushed past us, making my feet sink deeper into the sand. "About what's in here, I mean?"

"I've gotten bitten by crabs before," she said, "and stung by jellyfish. But it's not a big deal. And it doesn't happen very often."

The water was warm, but I felt a shiver go through me. "What about, um, sharks?"

Sammy hesitated. "We won't go very deep today, okay?"

So there *were* sharks.

You know you want to run, said the voice in my head. *Just do it. Run NOW!*

But I made myself stay put.

I am Miranda, I told the voice, *brave and bold. I do not run from danger.*

Sammy took another step forward, and, gripping her hand tight, I did too. The water was halfway to my knees.

"Maybe you should think about all the good things in the water," Sammy said. "All the friendly animals. Starfish, seahorses, turtles, dolphins."

"Okay," I said, thinking of Bluey, safely tucked under my sheets back in Sammy's bedroom. "I'll try."

Closing my eyes this time, I forced myself forward once more. The water rushed past my knees. When I opened my eyes, Sammy was beaming at me. "You're doing so great!"

"Thanks," I said, smiling back. "I guess it's not so—"

Just then a dark blob darted past my left foot. I screamed and, before I could stop myself, started sprinting for shore.

When I reached dry sand, my heart pounding, Jai and the girls were all staring at me. Feeling my cheeks go pink, I turned away and squinted at Sammy, who was trotting back through the surf, holding something in her hand.

"What is that?" I asked.

"What scared you," she said, lifting it up. It was a brownish green thing with lots of slimy tentacles.

"Is it an animal?" I asked, wrinkling my nose. "Is it dangerous?"

"It's *seaweed*!"

I peered closer. Even I knew that seaweed was about as dangerous as a cotton ball. Was *this* really what I had run from? Seaweed?

"Sorry," I mumbled. "I panicked."

"Don't be sorry!" Sammy protested. "You were awesome."

I was caught between shame and pride when Sammy launched the clump of seaweed at me. She giggled as I jumped to the left to avoid getting hit and the girls behind me shrieked. It took me a second to realize that Sammy wasn't laughing *at* me. She was just laughing because we were having fun. Together. I began to giggle, too, as I picked up the clump of seaweed and jiggled it in front of her face.

"Ew," I heard one of the girls mutter. "They are *so* weird."

Usually, hearing something like that would have made me feel sticky with embarassment.

But if Sammy was weird, I wasn't sure I wanted to be anything else.

12

After Sammy and I went into the water one more time (this time, I waded in almost to my waist), we ventured up the beach to see the sea turtle's nest. There wasn't a whole lot to look at—just four poles connected by a square of plastic ribbon that said Do Not Enter.

"There's, like, a hundred eggs down there," she said. "And when they hatch, the baby turtles will all go running across the beach into the ocean. Most of them die pretty soon, though. They're just too small. A lot of them get eaten. I guess that's why sea turtles have so many babies. So at least some of them will survive."

It made me sad, thinking of all those little turtles swimming around on their own with no one to protect them. It didn't seem fair. We turned away from the nest after just a couple of minutes, but all day I kept thinking about those eggs under the sand, waiting to hatch, and hoping that somehow all the babies inside would be okay.

After dinner that night, Aunt Clare dropped us off at the amusement park. We rode the bumper cars, then the carousel. After that, we stopped for cotton candy before getting into line for the Ferris wheel.

Just as the ride operator was closing our carriage door and I felt nervous butterfly wings beginning to tickle my stomach, someone slipped in. Caleb sat down across from us and smirked. My shoulders stiffened. The butterflies flapped faster.

"Caleb?" Sammy blurted. "What are you doing here? Did you, like, follow us or something?"

"No," he said. "I was already here, and then I saw you in line."

"But *why*?" Sammy asked. "And why are you here by yourself?"

I was just wondering if he had come over to pull some kind of prank on us when I saw an uncertainty flickering through his eyes that made me soften toward him, just a little. "All my friends are gone for the summer," he said, glancing at me and then quickly down again. "And home is just, uh, boring."

Sammy stared at him, eyes narrowed, as the Ferris

wheel lurched forward. I gripped the side of our carriage tight. "Yeah," she finally said. "Mine, too. That's why it's so awesome that Miranda is here."

She shot me a grateful look as we rocked higher.

"Where are you from, anyway?" Caleb asked, squinting into the setting sun. "Obviously not from around here." He nodded at my sunburned shoulders.

"Illinois," I said.

"This is her first time ever seeing the ocean," Sammy confided.

Caleb's brows shot up. "Really?"

"Look on a map," I grumbled. It wasn't *my* fault I'd never been to the beach before. "Illinois is landlocked."

"Well, that explains . . . some things," he said.

We were almost at the top of the wheel. You could see the whole Isle from here. Under the setting sun, everything was all peach bright and shimmery.

I looked beyond the Isle to the sea.

"Hey, what's that?" I asked, eyes landing on the little island with the lighthouse I had seen from Sammy's roof.

"That place?" Caleb said. "You sure you want to know about Keeper's Island?"

"What do you mean?"

"I can't believe I haven't told you yet!" Sammy said.

I sat up straighter. "Told me what?"

Caleb and Sammy glanced at each other.

"Nobody goes to Keeper's Island," he said. "Ever."

"Why?" I asked.

"Because it's haunted."

I felt my eyes widen.

"A long time ago, some pirates came to bury their treasure there," Sammy said. "But the treasure was cursed, so the lighthouse keeper didn't want it on his island. He tried to fight, but it was just him against all of them."

"So they killed him!" Caleb cried, plunging an invisible sword through the air. "And now his ghost haunts the island. Every ten years, he rises up from the grave and waits for an unsuspecting visitor. He still thinks he's protecting the island from pirates, see. The last victim got taken almost exactly ten years ago. Hasn't been seen since. He lived here on the Isle. Sailed out to Keeper's Island one summer day and never came back."

I turned to Sammy, suddenly remembering. "The man who lived in that old creepy house?" I asked. "We drove past it the first day, and you said he disappeared, but then your mom wouldn't let you finish the story."

"Yes! That's him. That's the one who got taken."

I was still kind of worried that Caleb was trying play some kind of prank on me, but Sammy wouldn't go along with it, would she? "Are you guys joking?"

They shook their heads. Sammy looked at me solemnly. "It's true," she said. "I swear."

I stared out at the island again, remembering how the darkened lighthouse had given me a strange feeling of dread the first time I saw it. Then, for just a second, over the tinkle of the carousel music, I could have sworn I heard a sharp cry carrying across the water. The hairs on the back of my neck rose.

"Did you guys hear that?" I asked. "That crying noise? It sounded like it was coming from Keeper's Island."

Caleb arched his eyebrows. "Well, like I said, it *has* been almost exactly ten years," he said. "The keeper's ghost is probably there, waiting for his next victim." He shrugged. "I didn't hear anything, though."

"Me either," said Sammy.

"I could have sworn—" I started, then stopped when I saw how Caleb was looking at me.

"It was probably just your imagination," he said. He glanced down at my knuckles, which were white from holding on to the side of the carriage so tight. "You're kind of scared of a lot of stuff, huh?"

"Shut up, Caleb," Sammy said.

"I'm not scared of anything," I huffed, forcing myself to loosen my fingers and fold my hands in my lap.

"Oh yeah?" Caleb said. "Then prove it."

My heart clattered in my chest. I knew I wasn't going

to like what came next, but how could I back down now? That's what old Miranda would have done. New Miranda would never shy away from a challenge.

"Fine," I said. "How?"

The last embers of sunlight glowed in his eyes. He licked his lips and leaned back on the bench, lacing his hands behind his head, like he was already really satisfied with himself. "Well, we can't get to Keeper's Island," he said. "But there *is* that abandoned house. The one where the old man lived before he was murdered."

"Yeah?" I asked. "What about it?"

A slow grin spread across Caleb's face.

13

"You don't have to do this, Miranda."

Sammy clutched my arm as we followed Caleb past the rows of beach cottages toward the abandoned house.

There was a buzzing in my ears like static on the radio, and I wasn't sure if it was the sound of the nearby tide coming in or of the blood pumping from my heart to my head.

"It's fine," I said lightly. "It's just a stupid dare."

From the corner of my eye, I saw Sammy bite down on her lower lip. She glanced back, in the direction of home.

I felt the tiniest flicker of satisfaction. For once, she was the uncertain one, the one who would rather be safe at home. *I* was the one ready for a little adventure.

Or at least I was pretending to be. I flipped my hair back behind my shoulder to complete the illusion.

"Seriously," Sammy whispered, "let's just go home and watch a movie or something. Who cares what Caleb thinks?"

Me, I thought. *I care.*

But there's this rule when you're twelve that you're not allowed to admit that you care what other people think about you. Like somehow caring makes you a fake.

So I couldn't just say that it would be nice if someone could look at me and see what they did when they looked at Sammy. Someone carefree and fearless.

"Nobody cares," I said instead. "It's just for fun."

And I sped up, shaking my arm free from her grip.

Soon the abandoned house loomed before us, guarded by a low iron fence and a set of gates in front of the walkway.

"How am I supposed to get in there?" I asked Caleb.

"Try the windows," he said. "I guess you could always break one."

"Miranda isn't breaking any windows," Sammy snapped.

"It's a big house. She'll find a way in somehow. Won't you, Miranda? And remember, you have to bring something back with you. That's the dare."

I stared up at the house. It glared back.

"This is so stupid," Sammy said. "Let's just—"

But I was already high-stepping over the little gates, and then I was marching down the cracked path and up the porch steps. The floorboards grunted under my feet. I wrapped my hand around the banister, but it was damp and wobbly.

Sammy and Caleb were having a hushed argument behind me, but I didn't turn around to see. Instead I moved toward the closest window. It was hidden behind a pair of shutters, which I pried apart. I tried to push the glass upward, but it didn't move.

There were three other first-floor windows that looked out toward the street, and I tried each one. The longer I stayed on the porch, the harder my knees began to buckle.

But none of the windows would budge.

Now what? I would have to walk around the house to the other first-floor windows. Or maybe there would be a back door. Or maybe Sammy was right, and we should just—

I stopped short. *The door!* I hadn't even thought about the front door. Probably because the chances of it being open all this time were zero, but still, it was worth a try, wasn't it?

I shuffled back to the center of the porch and pressed my thumb down against the door handle. I pushed.

And watched, wide-eyed, as the door slowly creaked open.

I stood there for a minute, staring into the inky house. I heard Caleb give a low whoop from the sidewalk.

All I had to do now was duck inside and find something to bring back, and then I would be done.

I darted through the door, hands fumbling ahead of me in the darkness. For a few seconds, I couldn't see anything and I fought to keep panic from rising up in my chest. Then a staircase came into view, straight in front of me. To either side, there was a doorway. I pitched myself through the one on the right and the next second had to swallow a cry as my shin collided with something hard.

"Ow," I whispered. "Ow, ow, ow."

Suddenly remembering my phone in my pocket, I pulled it out and turned on the flashlight app. A narrow cone of silver light illuminated the ground in front of me, and I saw that I had run into some kind of wooden box.

Shining the light farther into the room, I realized that it was filled with boxes like the one I had just crashed into. Some of them were stacked three high. They took up almost every bit of space that wasn't already claimed by what I figured must have been furniture, but I couldn't tell because it was all covered with sheets. I sniffed the air, and my nose was instantly filled with dust.

Just find something and get out.

The problem was, I couldn't see anything but boxes and furniture. I tried to lift the lid of the box closest to my feet, but it was sealed shut.

My shin and my heart both throbbed. It was too dark. Too quiet.

I whirled around, then scuttled through the other doorway I had seen. And found myself in a library.

Bingo.

But as I pulled a book from the nearest shelf, goose bumps sprouted up my arms. I froze.

I was sure I had seen a flicker of movement from the corner of the room.

Just a mouse.

I turned, slowly, shining the light across the library. There was a tall shape there—taller than me—with a sheet draped over it.

The ends of the sheet were rustling against the floorboards.

For a moment, I was too terrified to do or say anything.

Then, "Hello?" I croaked. "Is someone under there?"

There was no answer.

I could have just turned and run from the house. I'm not sure why I didn't, except that the terror of never knowing what was under that sheet felt somehow greater than the terror of finding out right then.

I took a step closer. And another. Then my hand was reaching out again, fingers wrapping around the thin cloth. I aimed the flashlight and pulled.

"Ladrão!" cawed the voice of whoever was hiding underneath.

I closed my eyes and screamed.

"Pega ladrão!" it cried. "Polícia!"

When I opened my eyes, I saw that the voice didn't belong to a person. It belonged to a bird.

The bird flapped furiously against the bars of its enormous cage, which was set atop a wooden stand. It squawked and bleated as it tried to force its beak and talons through the bars far enough to swipe at me.

Then there were more noises. Something thumping

against the ceiling. Footsteps coming down the stairs. A dog barking.

The footsteps stopped, and a light switched on.

"What in God's name is going on down here?" demanded a voice, this one unmistakably human. And unmistakably furious.

I spun around to see an old man in a bathrobe, with a snowy beard. A mangy brown dog was barking furiously at his feet.

"I—I'm sorry," I said. "I didn't mean to—I didn't know anyone was—"

"Here to interrupt your burglary?" he asked, his eyebrows arching. He held out his hand in a "stop" gesture to the dog, which went silent but kept its eyes pinned on me.

"I wasn't going to steal anything," I mumbled.

And in my defense, my friends told me you were dead.

His eyes flicked to the book I still held in my hand. "Oh?"

"I'm sorry," I said again, holding it out. "Really sorry."

He took the book. "I should call the police. That's what Safira wants me to do."

He walked over to the cage and held out a finger to the enormous blue bird, whose wings began to settle.

If he called the police, they would call Sammy's

parents. And Aunt Clare wouldn't be able to convince Uncle Amar not to call Mom this time. The Grovers wouldn't want a criminal staying in their house.

"Please," I begged, "please don't call them. I'll never come back, I swear. I'll never do it again. If you tell, my mom will—"

"Miranda!" Sammy called, hurtling through the door. "Are you okay? We heard a scream, and Caleb ran away, but—"

She stopped when she saw the old man. His eyes widened as they moved from me to Sammy and back to me. His gaze was intense, like an angry finger pressing against my chest. He must have been working out exactly what to do about the two of us, because he didn't say anything for a moment.

"Exactly how old are you two?" he asked. "Eleven?"

"Twelve," I said. "I'm twelve."

Was that old enough to be sent to juvenile detention?

"A bit young to be breaking and entering," he said coolly, as Sammy inched to my side. "You were saying something about your mother?"

"My mom, um, sent me here for the summer," I said, "because she has a really important job to do. And if you call the police, I'll have to go home and she won't be able to do it."

In the long, silent seconds that followed, I saw

something—pity, I thought—dart across his face.

Finally he lifted his chin, so that the tip of his beard pointed out instead of down. "I won't call the police," he said. "I won't tell anyone about this."

"Thank you," I breathed. "Thank you, thank you."

"Not so fast," he said, holding up a hand. "You've still trespassed on my property, and I can't just let you run off scot-free."

"You want us to, like . . . pay you?" Sammy asked.

He shot Sammy a funny look. "I'm a man of many interests," he said. "But blackmail is not one of them."

"Then what?" I asked.

He thought for another moment.

"As it happens," he said, "I've just returned from a very long trip. I have quite a lot to unpack and sort through." He gestured back toward the crates in the other room. "It's a big job for one person. I could use you two to help me."

"Three," said Sammy. "No way is Caleb getting off the hook, and no way are we coming back here alone."

"Fine," he said. "And you won't be alone. My housekeeper, Betsy, will be here, too."

I glanced around the dusty room, at the cobwebbed chandelier hanging from the ceiling. Either Betsy was the worst housekeeper in the world, or she hadn't started yet.

"Okay," I said. "Deal. We'll be here."

He considered me for another minute, like he was trying to decide whether or not he could trust me. Then he nodded. "Tomorrow," he said. "Three o'clock."

"Three o'clock," Sammy repeated. "Now, let's go."

She steered us from the room. The dog at the old man's feet growled as we passed.

"Thanks again, Mr. . . . um . . ."

"Taylor," he said. "My name is Taylor."

"Right. Thanks again, Mr. Taylor," I said. Then Sammy was pushing me out of the house, back into the fresh night air.

15

Uncle Amar and Aunt Clare were waiting on the porch for Sammy and me. They stood as we jogged up the steps, Uncle Amar draping an arm around Aunt Clare.

"It's almost ten o'clock, Sammy," he said. I had never heard his voice sound so harsh. "You were supposed to be home by nine. We've been really worried."

"I'm sorry," Sammy said. "I texted you to say we'd be a little late."

"And I texted you to say you needed to come home," said Aunt Clare.

"It was my fault," I muttered.

Sammy glanced at me and gave me the slightest shake of her head. But I already knew what the Grovers thought of me. What did I have to lose by taking the blame, as long as they didn't find out the truth?

"I, um, lost my phone," I said.

"Yeah," said Sammy. "We had to go all around the park looking for it."

"It was in the bathroom."

Sammy's parents looked at each other, then back at us. I could tell they weren't sure whether to believe us or not. But I could also tell they didn't want to accuse me of being a liar.

"Fine," Aunt Clare said. "But you're not going out at night again. And tomorrow, you'll be helping cook *and* do dishes. Sammy can help Amar with dinner, and Miranda, you can make dessert."

"Yes, Mom," said Sammy flatly.

"Yes, Aunt Clare," I echoed.

I gulped. What was I going to make? I would have to figure something out. Now was not the time to come clean about my lack of baking experience. Then Aunt Clare would *know* I was a liar. Besides, if I could pull off a decent dessert, maybe she and Uncle Amar would start to change their minds about me.

When we got to Sammy's room, she flung herself onto her bed, facing the wall. For a minute, the only sound was Jai talking on the phone in the next room.

"I'm really sorry I got us in trouble," I said. I sat down on the corner of the bed.

For a few seconds, she didn't move. Then she sat up and brushed the hair from her face. I saw a tear sneaking its way from her eye.

"Are you crying?" I asked, alarmed.

"Yes, Miranda," she said, taking a big stuffed polar bear in her arms and resting her chin on it in a pout. "You were pretty mean before. I told you you shouldn't go into that place, and you ignored me, and then you were screaming, and I thought something really bad had happened to you. And now we have to spend our summer cooped up in some creepy old house."

I dropped my head so she wouldn't see the pink spreading over my cheeks. I had been so busy trying to prove myself to Caleb that I hadn't even cared how Sammy felt. I'd almost gotten us arrested, and now I had ruined her summer.

So much for the new and improved Miranda. No matter who I tried to be, I always seemed to ruin things.

"Are *you* crying now?" Sammy asked.

"No," I said, wiping away the evidence too late. "I'm just embarrassed. I was trying to—to—"

"To what?"

"To be more like you, I guess," I admitted. "You make everything look so easy and fun."

She snorted. "If you think that, you should see me in math class," she said. "I'm one of the worst in my grade. People make fun of me because they say Indians are supposed to be good at math."

The warmth in my cheeks turned to hot anger. "That's so not okay," I said, stuffing Bluey into my arms. "Aren't there, like, more than a billion Indians in the world? Do people think they're all just the same? They can't all be good at math. That's just simple statistics."

Sammy shot me a narrow smile. "See?" she said. "You're probably really good at math."

Math *was* my best subject, but now didn't seem like a very good time to tell Sammy that. Besides, I was still fuming about what she had told me. "That's why middle school sucks," I said. "If there's anything different or special about you, kids make fun of you for it. I for one think you're awesome. And anybody who can't see that is nuts."

"Thanks, Miranda," Sammy said.

"And I'm so sorry I ruined your summer."

She reached over and gave me a small shove.

"You didn't ruin my summer," she said. "So what if we have to spend a couple hours every day trapped in a room with Caleb Dillworth and some grumpy old guy?"

"Won't your mom wonder where we are?" I asked. "If we tell her about Mr. Taylor, she'll want to know how we met him. Or she'll want to meet him herself, and then he'll tell her all about us breaking in and she'll tell my mom."

"Don't worry," Sammy said. "She has her piano lessons in the afternoon. And if she asks what we've been doing while she's gone, I'll just tell her we went to the library to do research for my story. It'll be okay. Actually, it'll be better. Because we'll find a way to make it fun."

This time, I actually believed her.

16

When we got to the harbor for our sailing lesson the next day, Jason instructed us to get life jackets on.

Life jackets meant we were going out on the water.

I took a deep breath. So maybe breaking into Mr. Taylor's house last night hadn't been the best start to the new and improved Miranda, but that didn't mean I was giving up on changing.

You can do this, I told myself firmly.

Caleb was already on the beach, toeing some kind of design in the sand. Sammy stalked up to him and ruined it with a swift kick.

"Hey!"

"Hey yourself," she said. "I can't believe you left us last night."

He shrugged and shuffled his feet. "I didn't want to get in trouble."

"It was *your* idea," I said, surprised at my own boldness. "If anyone should be in trouble, it's you."

Even more surprisingly, Caleb didn't fight back. "I'm sorry, okay?" he said. "What happened, anyway? After I left?"

"What happened is that the old man who lives there—key word being *lives*—told us we had to come back and help him unpack all these boxes," said Sammy, "starting today at three. You'll be there, or I'll tell your mom everything."

He winced at the mention of his mom. "Don't," he said quietly.

"Then we'll see you at three," Sammy replied.

He aimed a lazy kick of his own at the sand. "Whatever. Not like there's anything else to do around here anyway."

Sammy turned on her heel, and I followed her to grab our life jackets from the shed.

"Is Caleb one of the kids from school?" I asked. "Who make fun of you?"

Sammy glanced up. "Well, he did back in elementary school," she said. Then she cocked her head. "Actually, he hasn't really bothered me this year. Some of his friends still do, though."

I linked my arm through hers. "Well, if he says anything mean," I said, "it'll be two against one."

Being brave wasn't just about overcoming your own fears, I decided. It was about standing up for your friends, too.

Sammy smiled. "I like the sound of that."

Jason was on the beach now, waving us over. Once I was standing in front of him, he took the straps of my life jacket and jerked them as tight as they would go. "No way you can sink now," he said, winking.

I really wished he hadn't said the word "sink."

Jason instructed Sammy and Caleb to get into one boat (they both rolled their eyes) and helped me get into another. As he pushed it out into the water, I clung to its edges until my knuckles were as white as the plastic. I hated the way the boat bobbed on the waves and made me feel like we were going to tip over any second.

"We'll stay right here today," Jason said, "where it's nice and shallow. See?"

He pointed over the edge of the boat, into the water below. It was turquoise, but somehow it was also clear enough to see straight to the sandy bottom. It didn't look any deeper than a few feet. As I stared, a little school of shiny fish flickered past.

Then Jason told me to start unfurling the sail, and suddenly there were lots of things to do—ropes to cleat, a tiller to steer with, the boom to look out for. So many things to think about that, for a while, I forgot to think about how scared I was.

17

After our lesson, Aunt Clare told me to make her a grocery list with all the things I would need to make dessert that night. Thinking of the peach stands we'd seen on our drive from the airport, I searched online to find the recipe for the mile-high peach pie that I had in my binder at home. It seemed like a simple enough choice, but I was still nervous about trying it.

Nervous is okay, I told myself. On *Baking Battles,* the contestants who got eliminated first were almost always the ones who were really confident.

Before leaving for her piano lessons, Aunt Clare asked Sammy what we were going to do that afternoon, and Sammy told her we were going to the library to look at some books on turtles. I was surprised, and kind of impressed, at how easy it seemed for her to lie like that.

Then, a few minutes before three, Sammy and I started toward Mr. Taylor's. When we got there, Caleb was already standing at the edge of the lawn, waiting.

The house didn't look quite so creepy in the day-time, but it *did* look even more run-down in the bright afternoon sun. There were shingles missing from the roof, which leaned to one side, and posts knocked out from under the porch banister. At least today the iron gates were open.

Next door, a woman took a break from watering her yard to stare at us.

"We'd better go knock," I said finally, "or we'll be late."

But just as we reached the top of the creaking porch steps, the front door flew open, revealing an older woman with wild spirals of silver hair framing her round face.

"You must be our helpers," she said, beaming. "So kind of you to volunteer to come and lend a hand like this."

I shot a questioning look at Sammy. *Volunteer?* That wasn't exactly the word I would have used.

Still, it meant that Mr. Taylor had kept his end of our bargain. He hadn't told anyone about the break-in.

"I'm Betsy," she said, wiping her hand on her floral apron and then extending it. Caleb and Sammy shook hands and introduced themselves. Then it was my turn.

"Miranda," Betsy mused, studying me. "Such a pretty name. You never hear that one anymore. Your mother must have very good taste."

"Thanks," I said.

"Well, don't just stand out there. That heat is unbearable. Come in, come in!"

She ushered us inside the house, which was a bit cooler than outside but still pretty stuffy. Rays of sunlight shooting through the windows revealed thousands of tiny dust particles swirling around each other like couples waltzing at a tiny ball.

"We've got guests!" Betsy called upstairs. Then she turned to us. "I'll just go get you some lemonade from the kitchen."

She plucked her way through the maze of crates and living-room furniture—which, I saw, had been uncovered since last night—and disappeared, leaving us alone in the entryway.

"Sammy," I said, "remember yesterday? We saw those guys carrying a bunch of crates to a truck in the harbor."

"What's in them?" Caleb asked, wrinkling his nose. "Something smells funky."

{ 100 }

"It might just be the house," said Sammy. "Nobody's been taking care of this place for ten years."

We all startled as a voice came from the library.

"Ladrão! Ladrão!" it squawked. "Polícia! Pega ladrão!"

"Whoa," breathed Caleb, brushing past us and striding toward the birdcage in the corner, where the parrot that had scared me the night before glared at us as it cawed. "It's huge."

We hovered in the doorway of the library. I had been so scared the night before that I hadn't really gotten a proper look at the parrot. It was even more enormous than I'd realized—probably three feet from the tip of its tail to its head—and had dark blue feathers, a long gray beak, and steely talons. The feathers around its eyes and the bottom of its beak were bright yellow, while the eyes themselves were coal black.

"What's your name, little dude?" Caleb said, holding out his fingers.

The bird opened its beak and fluttered its giant wings. "Polícia!" it cried.

"Is it speaking French?" I asked.

"Portuguese, actually," said another voice. We turned to see Mr. Taylor standing at the bottom of the stairs behind us. "And I'd be careful with those fingers, young man. Hyacinth macaws have some of the strongest beaks in the bird kingdom, and this one was trained as a guard parrot. That's why she's shouting for someone to call the police."

Caleb jerked his fingers away from the bars as Mr. Taylor brushed past us. He strode to the cage and murmured something we couldn't understand. Then he handed the bird a stick from a pile under the cage. She took it in her beak and instantly snapped it in two.

Caleb's eyes went wide.

"She's so big," Sammy murmured.

"Hyacinth macaws are the biggest parrots in the world," Mr. Taylor said, clearing his throat. "Well, the New Zealand kakapo can be heavier, but since the kakapo can't fly, I think we'll let that honor stay with Safira and her kind."

"Is she yours?" I asked.

"In a manner of speaking," Mr. Taylor said. In the daylight, I saw that the skin above his beard was deeply tanned and flecked with bits of white and red and charcoal. He had wispy hair, with a clump sticking up like a tuft of grass growing from a crack in the sidewalk. He considered me with gray eyes.

"I met her owner in Brazil. She was my landlord, in fact. In a town called Ouro Preto. It means Black Gold. Most of the world has forgotten it now, but back in the eighteenth century, during the Brazilian gold rush, it was the biggest city anywhere in the Americas.

"Anyway, Safira's owner was an old woman, and

she didn't have long to live. She wasn't a very nice old lady, truth be told, and she had no family or friends left who would care for Safira after she died. She asked me to take Safira with me when I left, and I agreed."

"That's where you've been all this time?" Sammy asked. "Brazil?"

"I've been in Brazil," he said. "And everywhere else, too. Wherever the wind blew me, that's where I sailed."

"You've been on a boat?" I asked. "For ten years?"

"Off and on. The sea can make a very good companion."

I pursed my lips. We would have to agree to disagree.

Then I remembered the big boat I had seen sailing into the harbor my first morning on August Isle. The *Albatross*. It must be Mr. Taylor's.

"Well, I think we'll make a start now," he said.

As we passed by the staircase, we heard a clacking noise and looked up to see the dog from the night before standing at the top of the stairs. Except today it wore a huge cone around its neck, and when it stumbled to the bottom of the steps, it turned and found its cone stuck in the doorway of the living room. Caleb caught my eye, and we had to look away to keep from laughing as the dog started to bark. Mr. Taylor grumbled something and tugged its cone in the right direction.

We followed them into the living room, where, squashed in among all the crates, were a red-and-blue-plaid sofa, a coffee table, and an armchair. Across from the sofa was a dark fireplace. The walls were decorated with pretty paintings of the beach, but something was missing from the room.

After a second, I realized what it was. There were no photographs sitting in frames on the mantel, or books on the coffee table. So even though the room was full, it felt empty, too.

Betsy appeared from a swinging door, carrying a tray with a pitcher, four glasses, and cookies that looked homemade. Sammy clucked her tongue at the dog. But it didn't even look up. Instead it flopped down on the floor at Mr. Taylor's feet.

"He can't hear you," Mr. Taylor said. "He's deaf. Found him on the streets on Kárpathos, one of the Greek islands. I gave him one scrap of fish, and suddenly I had a new shadow. He followed me everywhere I went for the rest of my stay. Including onto my boat when it was time to go."

"What's his name?" Sammy asked. "And what's the cone for?"

"I've always just called him Skilos. That's Greek for 'dog.' And he had a little operation this morning. The cone is to keep him from licking his wound."

Sammy knelt beside him as Betsy set her tray down

on the coffee table. "No offense," Sammy muttered, "but it seems like he deserves a better name than Dog."

One of Mr. Taylor's scraggly eyebrows rose, but he didn't reply.

"You have kind of a thing for saving animals, huh?" I asked.

"Do you have any other pets?" Caleb asked eagerly. "Like a boa constrictor? Or a Komodo dragon?"

A sound of deep disgust rose up from Betsy's throat. "I'll thank you not to give him any more ideas," she said. "Two strays are plenty. The last thing we need is one with scales."

"I did see Komodo dragons when I was in Indonesia," Mr. Taylor said, considering. "I don't think they'd make very good pets, though."

"I'll leave you to it," Betsy said. "I'll be in the kitchen cleaning out the cabinets if you need anything."

"Well then," said Mr. Taylor, coughing to clear some of the pebbles from his voice.

"You, reptile boy, what's your name?"

"Caleb."

"Caleb." Mr. Taylor picked up a hammer from the top of one of the crates and handed it to him. "Use the hammer claws to pull the nails out of the crate lids."

"Cool," Caleb said.

"Once you've done that, you'll be in charge of pulling all the books out of them, too. Some of them I'll be donating, and some I'll be keeping. You'll take the keepers into my library and shelve them."

Caleb scrunched up his nose, clearly disappointed with the second half of his assignment.

"And Sammy, wasn't it?" asked Mr. Taylor.

Sammy nodded.

"In each one of these crates, there'll be a stack of pictures. You're in charge of pulling them out and putting them into those scrapbooks." He pointed to a teetering pile of leather binders sitting on a stack of crates. Sammy's eyes bulged. How many pictures did he mean?

"What about me?" I asked. "What do I do?"

He flicked his gaze to me. He was tall and wide chested, and something about him reminded me of the August Oak. He raised an eyebrow. "How are you at typing?"

"Which one should we do first?" I asked, staring at the infestation of wooden crates.

"Whichever you like," Mr. Taylor said. "Pick one."

He settled on the opposite end of the sofa from me and opened a notebook. I pointed to the nearest crate, and Caleb began to pry out the nails. At first, all I could see inside was crumpled newspaper. The articles were all written in a different language.

Then I dug into the box and pulled out a pair of wooden clogs.

"Aha!" Mr. Taylor barked. "I see we're starting with Holland. I've been missing those."

He gestured for me to hand the clogs over, then slid

them onto his feet with a contented sigh.

"Do they really wear wooden shoes in Holland?" Sammy asked.

"When they're at home, or working in the garden, certainly," Mr. Taylor said. "The older generations wear them when they go out, too."

An ancient laptop sat between us on the couch.

"Should I be writing this down?" I asked, gesturing to it.

"No," he said. "Not yet. What's next?"

Next was a book of very old maps, bound in leather, which I handed carefully to Caleb. Then came a stack of pictures, which Sammy took. Then my hands closed around something tall and narrow in the box. Some kind of framed picture, with more sheets of newspaper taped around it.

Mr. Taylor rubbed his hands together. "Ah, yes," he said. "Please. Open it."

I tore away the newspaper to reveal a framed picture of an odd flower, striped red and white.

"Now, this is really quite special," he said, taking the painting from me. His eyes shone as he studied it.

"It looks like a painting of a flower to me," Caleb said. "Is that what's in all these boxes? Just boring stuff like books and paintings and shoes?"

Mr. Taylor lowered the painting and stared at Caleb for such a long moment that Caleb's cheeks began to go red under the old man's gaze. I took a nervous sip of lemonade.

"I am not a collector of *stuff*, young man," he said. A growl shadowed his words. "These boxes are filled with *stories*. Forgotten stories, or rather stories that are in danger of being forgotten. Stories that should be remembered."

"What do you mean?" Sammy asked.

Mr. Taylor narrowed his eyes at Caleb, then released him from his gaze. "I'll tell you. Just let me find the right page." He thumbed through the journal in his hand. "Miranda, this is where you come in. As I read, you'll transcribe, all right? I wrote all the stories out by hand because I'm no good with technology, but now I need them typed."

"Okay," I said, gathering up the laptop. My fingers hovered over the keyboard. "Ready."

Mr. Taylor cleared his throat.

While I was walking through the Dutch country-side one March afternoon, I became lost just as a storm broke overhead. The wind blew so hard that I could barely walk, and the raindrops were like needles piercing my skin. Soon I was soaked to the bone and numb with cold.

I happened to be passing by a tulip farm, where I spied a farmhouse at the end of a field splashed with the brightest yellows, the most shocking oranges, and the fiercest reds. Seeking shelter, I battled my way to the door and knocked.

A woman answered who had tulips even in her cheeks. She beckoned me into the house, took my coat to dry against the furnace, and sat me down in a chair by just the kind of roaring fire I had hoped I might find inside. Presently her husband came in, spoke a few words with her in Dutch, and sat down in the chair opposite me. His wife brought us warm bread, smoked cheese, and hot tea.

We began to talk about his tulip crop, and his farm, which had been in his family for many generations. And finally, he told me the story of the broken tulip.

"The Dutch have always been—and will always be—crazy for tulips," he said. "During the Second World War, tulips saved many families from starvation, did you know? They ate the bulbs.

"But perhaps we never loved them so much as in the seventeenth century. Back then, only the wealthy could afford to plant them in their gardens. And the most prized tulip of all was the Semper Augustus. It was what they called a *broken tulip—a tulip that has broken into two colors. In the case of the Semper Augustus, the bloom was striped white and crimson. The country went mad for it. But there was only one man who bred them, and he had only twelve bulbs. He refused to sell any of them, although he was offered enough money to buy a grand house for a single specimen.*

"In the end, the tulip fever died down and the Semper Augustus simply disappeared. Many years later, we learned that its striping was actually caused by a disease. The very thing that made it so beautiful was what would eventually kill it.

"As a child, I used to think this story very sad. Why would nature offer something so beautiful only to take it away again? But as I grew older, I realized that the Semper Augustus was a reminder that often the most exquisite things are the first to fade away." Here he pointed up to a painting I had not noticed before, of a tulip with peppermint petals, just like he had described. "And life is the most exquisite thing of all. So we must never take it for granted."

Finishing his story, the farmer then asked how I had come to be in Holland. Once the storm passed, I thanked the couple and took my leave.

When I looked back at the farmhouse, they were still on the front stoop, waving. Looking over their heads, I caught the last threads of an enormous rainbow before it shimmered away.

"That's such a cool story," said Sammy.

"It's kind of sad," I replied. "I feel sorry for that poor flower."

I thought I would rather look at the pretty beach painting over Mr. Taylor's mantel than the one of the Semper Augustus.

"I feel sorry for the guy who could have bought a mansion," said Caleb with a snort.

Mr. Taylor ignored him. "You see, whenever I met someone on my travels, I asked them to give me a story. Something that they wanted to be preserved."

"How did you get them to give you the painting?" I asked. "Doesn't the man miss it?"

"As it turned out, the artist was the man's wife. She had painted the picture from a sketch of the flower she'd seen in a museum. I asked her if she would paint another for me, just like the one over their mantel, and she agreed. I returned for it some weeks later."

"Did it cost a lot of money?" Caleb asked.

Sammy jabbed him in the ribs.

"It didn't cost me a cent," Mr. Taylor said. "Only a story of my own, and a promise that I would make sure the story of the Semper Augustus was remembered."

"Can we hear your story?" I asked. "The one you traded them?"

He shook his head. "Not right now," he said. "Now, I think we should eat Betsy's cookies before they get cold and she scolds me for working you too hard."

I passed the plate of cookies around and we each nibbled in silence. As soon as I was done, I turned back to Mr. Taylor. "Can we do another box now?"

When it was time to go, Betsy came out from the kitchen to say goodbye and tripped over the dog. He scrambled up and immediately got his cone stuck between two crates. Sammy giggled as she helped him through. Then he found a sunny spot of rug and went back to sleep.

"I've never seen a dog so lazy," Betsy said. "He's more like a slug than a dog."

"That's it!" Sammy said, reaching out and scratching the dog under his floppy ears. He didn't wake up. "Slug! That can be his name!"

"Slug the dog?" I asked.

"It's quite fitting," said Mr. Taylor. "Slug it is."

He walked us to the door.

"See you tomorrow," I said.

"Looking forward to it," he replied.

"Me too," I said. And I realized I meant it.

19

"Well, *that wasn't quite* as boring as I thought it was going to be," Caleb said, as we walked away from Mr. Taylor's house.

"It was actually kind of cool, wasn't it?" Sammy said.

"Yeah," I replied. "And Mr. Taylor isn't mean like I thought he would be. He's just a little . . ."

"Strange?" Sammy finished.

"Yeah," I said. "But not really in a bad way."

We came to the end of the block and paused. A few seconds ticked by. Then, "Well," Sammy said, "we need to get home. We have to help my dad make dinner."

"What are you making?" Caleb asked.

Sammy and I glanced at each other. Why did Caleb care what we were having for dinner?

"Pakora kadhi," she said. "It's kind of like vegetable fritters in this yellow curry sauce."

I tensed as I waited for Caleb to say something. What if he cracked a joke about the food?

"I've never had Indian food before," he said.

"I make it spicy," Sammy replied.

"I love spicy food," he said.

Sammy and I glanced at each other again. He wasn't making fun of her. He was trying to score an invite to her house for dinner.

"Fine," Sammy said. "You can come. But you have to dice the onion."

Caleb grinned, and suddenly I noticed that he had a nice smile. It lifted higher on the left than on the right, and he had this tiny gap between his front two teeth that was kind of cute. He caught me looking at him, and I darted my gaze away.

Caleb texted his mom as we walked back to Sammy's to tell her where he was going, and Aunt Clare didn't seem to mind having an unexpected guest show up for dinner. "The more the merrier," she said, waving us into the kitchen. "How was the library? You didn't bring any books home?"

Caleb looked at us with raised eyebrows but said nothing.

"We mostly did research on the computers," Sammy replied smoothly. "We ran into Caleb there, too."

We walked into the kitchen just as Uncle Amar finished tying his apron strings. He reached out to shake Caleb's right hand while Sammy thrust an onion into his left. "Here. I'll start making the batter for the pakoras."

"And I'll help Miranda with her pie," Aunt Clare said.

I took out my phone to pull the recipe up and saw that I had missed a call from Dad and a text from Mom. I must have forgotten to switch the ringer back on that morning.

Mom's message was a picture of her standing at the top of a mountain, arms outstretched, grinning into the camera.

Hugs from Argentina.

she had written underneath.

"Is that from your mom?" Aunt Clare asked, looking over my shoulder. "She looks like she's having a great time! Tell her we say hello."

She did look like she was having a great time. Just like she had in Aunt Clare's pictures.

Trying to ignore how my chest was suddenly tightening, I typed back a quick response and pulled up the pie recipe. Across the kitchen, Sammy and Caleb seemed to be fighting about how finely he needed to dice the onion while Uncle Amar made the dough for the chapatis, a kind of Indian flatbread. Aunt Clare was still waiting for me to tell her what to do.

"Um," I said. "Maybe you could start by chopping the peaches?"

She looked at me quizzically. "Shouldn't I peel them first?"

"Oh, yeah," I said. "That's what I meant. And I'll do the crust."

"You're the boss," she said, handing me an apron.

While Aunt Clare peeled the peaches, I measured out the flour and salt for the crust. The recipe said to cut the butter into little squares and to mix it into the flour, so I started on that next.

It took a long time to cut two sticks of butter into squares, and my mind kept straying from what my hands were doing to Mom's text. I always thought that when I finally made my first pie, Mom would be standing beside me, not on some mountain in Argentina.

But now I wondered why I'd even let myself imagine such a thing. Mom had never baked anything except cookies from a roll of dough. And when I had asked her if we could make a pie or a cake together, she always had some kind of excuse. Strawberries weren't in season. She was too tired to go to the grocery store. The oven was on the fritz. Once, we bought all the stuff we needed to make an apple tart, but then Mom took a last-minute assignment, and by the time she got back, Dad had eaten most of the apples.

Maybe all this time, Mom had been wishing for me to be someone I wasn't. But what if I had been wishing for *her* to be somebody she wasn't, too?

By the time I had added the butter to the flour, and then the vinegar, and mixed it together into a dough, the pakoras were simmering on the stove, delicious coils of steam rising from the pan. Caleb had gone to try to play guitar with Jai, and Sammy was helping Uncle Amar with the kadhi—the curry sauce.

"Okay," I said, wiping my wrist against my hot brow as I consulted the recipe. "Now I have to— Oh no."

"What is it?" Aunt Clare asked.

I bit my lip. The pie dough was supposed to chill in the refrigerator for at least an hour. Then it would be in the oven for another hour, and cooling for thirty minutes after that. At this rate, we wouldn't be eating dessert until midnight. Why hadn't I read the recipe more carefully? Why didn't they ever show the chilling part on *Baking Battles*?

"Nothing," I said hastily. I had just remembered a trick from the show that might work.

I filled a glass with ice water, then dipped my fingers in before I began shaping the dough into two rounds— one for the bottom of the pie and one for the top. Cold as my fingers were, I could still feel heat rising in my cheeks as I tried to roll the dough. It was supposed to flatten into a perfect quarter-inch-thick circle.

Instead it stuck stubbornly to my hands and to the rolling pin.

Aunt Clare glanced over my shoulder. "Why don't you try some more flour?" she asked.

But no amount of flour would make the dough lie flat. The harder I tried, the harder it became to roll. Finally Aunt Clare lifted the rolling pin from my hands.

"You haven't done this before, huh?" she said. Her voice was soft, not angry or annoyed.

I hung my head. "No," I admitted. "I've never made anything before. I just watch a lot of baking shows. They make it look so easy."

She brushed a bit of dried dough from my nose. "It's never as easy as it looks. That's why I don't bake. Amar's mother tried once to teach me to make chapatis. It's not very complicated. But I nearly burned her kitchen down, and I haven't been allowed in since."

I smiled, just a little. "I think when you said you wanted to be a baker," she went on, "I assumed you knew how. But that was silly of me."

I looked around. The counter was dusted in flour and flecked with butter. Measuring cups and spoons were strewn across it. All I had wanted was to prove that I could do something useful, and instead I had turned the kitchen into a disaster zone.

"I could have told you," I said. "Now I've made a huge mess, and there's nothing for dessert."

Aunt Clare twisted her lips in thought. Then her eyes lit up. "Well," she said, "there is *one* thing we can try."

"It's really good," I said as I took my second bite of the pakora kadhi. Sammy *had* made it spicy. But the sauce was creamy and kind of sour, too, and the combination was mouthwateringly delicious.

"It's my great-grandmother's recipe," Uncle Amar said. "She was famous for it."

"Have you been to India?" Caleb asked Sammy.

"Yeah. Once when I was a baby, and once last summer."

"Did you like it?" I asked.

"Well, I don't remember anything from the first trip, obviously," she said. "But I liked the second one. Most of it, anyway. I got to see my dadi—my grandmother—and all these aunties and uncles and a bunch of cousins I didn't even know I had."

"They live in Mumbai," Jai said. "It's the biggest city in India. Like, way bigger than New York City. But our family is Punjabi. We're originally from Punjab, this region in northern India."

I was surprised to hear Jai speak so much. He usually didn't really talk at the dinner table, unless it was to argue with Sammy.

"What's it like?" I asked.

Jai and Sammy took turns telling us about their trip, and for a few minutes they seemed to forget how much they liked fighting with each other. They told us about their dadi's apartment, and how if you went to the roof of her building, you could just see a sliver of sea between the skyscrapers around it. They told us about the busy bazaars their aunties took them to, where Sammy bought a bunch of salwar kameez sets to wear and Jai found a stack of comic books in Punjabi.

"Does your family there speak English?" Caleb asked.

"Yeah. Most people in India speak at least some English," Jai said. "But there's also, like, a ton of different Indian languages. Our family speaks Punjabi, but also Hindi and some Marathi, too, because those are more common in Mumbai."

"Whoa," said Caleb. "That's a lot of languages."

"Can you guys speak any of those?" I asked.

Sammy and Jai shook their heads, and for a second I was worried that I had said something wrong because everyone was quiet.

Then Uncle Amar cleared his throat. "Sammy, maybe after dinner you can show Miranda the salwar kameez sets you brought back," he said.

Sammy brightened again. "And I'll teach you to

do bhangra—this really fun style of Punjabi dance. Maybe we'll watch a Bollywood movie, too!"

"I was in a Bollywood film once," said Uncle Amar, pointing his fork across the table at Caleb and me. "It was right after we moved to Mumbai. The director wanted to make me a star. He was very insistent. But I told him, not me, no thank you. I'm more than just a pretty face with great rhythm, you know. I've got brains, I said, and I'm going to use them to help people."

Jai snorted. "Dadi told me last time she came to visit that you were just an extra," he said. "She said you only got to be in the movie because a friend who knew the director owed you a favor. And that you were so bad they had to cut the scene you were in."

"Psh," Uncle Amar said, flicking his wrist. "You know how your dadi tells stories. You can't listen to anything she says."

When dinner was done, Aunt Clare brought over the peach cobbler she had helped me make by pouring the pie filling into the bottom of a baking pan, then covering it with dollops of my sticky dough.

"I thought you were making a pie," Caleb said as Aunt Clare set the cobbler down.

"We decided cobbler was better for tonight," she said. "It's lighter than pie." She sent me the slightest of winks.

"Wow!" exclaimed Sammy through her first bite. "It's so good!"

I plunged my fork into my own bowl and speared a bite. The way the cinnamon and peach flavors dissolved on my tongue reminded me of the sunset melting into the sea.

"It *is* good!" I said.

"It's excellent," said Uncle Amar, beaming. "You know, there's always a pie contest at the August Festival. You should enter this year."

"Yes! You totally should!" Sammy agreed.

"What's the August Festival?" I asked.

"It's this thing we do at the start of August every year," Caleb said. "It's to celebrate the anniversary of the town getting founded."

"I don't know," I said. "I don't think I'm good enough for that."

Aunt Clare gazed at me from across the table. "Oh yes, you are," she said.

I suddenly felt a surge of gratitude so strong that I found myself staring down at my plate, blinking back tears.

After Caleb went home, Sammy and I each picked our favorite salwar kameez from her closet and tried it on. They were outfits of loose pants, flowy tops, and a scarf called a dupatta that we slung over our shoulders. Mine was blue and gray, Sammy's bright pink and green. Then she tried to teach me one of the bhangra dances her cousins had taught her, which involved a lot of bouncing around on the balls of our feet and waving our arms in different motions. I kept bumping into her, though, and after a while we fell onto the bed, laughing.

When she went to brush her teeth, I called Dad. He answered on the first ring.

"Kiddo!" he said brightly. "I was just thinking about you."

"Hi, Dad," I said. The sound of his voice made me happy and sad all at once. Dad was the one person in the world I was sure never thought of me as a burden, and I felt a sudden desire to throw my arms around him and squeeze him tight. I settled for Bluey instead. "How's the case?"

"Oh, it's fine. I'm in Chicago right now. I'm about to have some pizza for dinner. Don't worry, though. I wouldn't dream of getting Hawaiian without you."

"I made a peach—er—cobbler for dessert tonight," I said.

"Hey, that's wonderful!" Dad replied. "I can't wait to taste some when you get home. Sounds like you're having a good time, huh?"

I hesitated, staring down at Bluey's one eye. I was dying to tell Dad about Mr. Taylor and Safira and

Slug. "I'm taking sailing lessons," I blurted instead.

"Wow. That's a bit—different for you," he said. "Do you like it?"

"I'm starting to," I said. "But don't tell Mom, okay? I want it to be a surprise."

"You got it. I think that's great, Miranda. I'm really proud of you. I miss you."

My chest swelled. "I miss you too, Dad."

After I hung up, Sammy was too tired to watch a movie, so we got into bed. But once again, I couldn't sleep. I listened to the muffled sound of Jai talking on the phone for a while before I finally crept out the porch door and up the stairs to the roof.

It was nice up there, with the warm sea breeze rustling through the palm fronds and blowing my hair into tangles. I liked the way it tasted on my tongue as I stared down at the winking lights of the Isle.

The moonlight shimmered over the ocean, and the sky was crammed full of stars. They looked bright beside the white moon, winking like fireflies. Just like the ones Batty and I had caught in our jar. For some reason, they made me think of Mom, and thinking of Mom made me feel sad again. I stood up to go back inside, but as I did, the air went suddenly still. Without the whisper of the palm trees, everything was quiet but the surf.

And then I heard it—the same sound I had heard

on the Ferris wheel the night before—coming from the direction of Keeper's Island. A shrill shriek that threw chills down my spine.

As I stared out at the dark patch in the sea, my breath caught in my throat.

No matter what Caleb said, I knew I wasn't imagining the sound.

And I *definitely* wasn't imagining the orange light that had suddenly blinked to life at the top of the abandoned lighthouse.

20

The next day, I decided not to say anything to Sammy or Caleb about what had happened on the roof. I didn't want them to think I was making stuff up.

And besides, it felt in some strange way like the island had been calling out to me, trying to tell me something. To send me a message.

But what that message was, I hadn't the slightest clue.

No way was I going to try to explain *that* to Caleb and Sammy. They would think I was totally nuts.

But I couldn't stop thinking about Keeper's Island the next morning, all through our sailing lesson and even as we found ourselves walking back to Mr.

Taylor's house that afternoon. Sammy skipped along, singing, while Caleb followed behind us.

He hadn't spoken very much that morning, and when I glanced over my shoulder, he was walking with his head down, kicking stray pebbles in his path.

Mr. Taylor opened the door as we climbed the porch stairs, and Slug trotted out. He didn't bark at us this time. Instead—after getting his cone caught in the doorway again—he went straight to Sammy and rolled over onto his back. She scratched his belly and behind his ears as Caleb and I stepped inside.

"Hi, kids," Mr. Taylor said. "Come on in. Watch your step."

He pointed to a bucket filled with gray water that had a mop sticking out of it. The house smelled strongly like lemon.

We looked up as Betsy appeared at the top of the stairs. "Hi, Miranda!" she called. "Hi, Caleb, Sammy! I'll come down in a few minutes and get you some key lime pie, okay?"

"I've never had key lime pie before," I said. I had only seen it on *Baking Battles*.

Caleb stared at me like I had just said I'd never been in a car. "You've never had key lime pie?"

"They probably don't have key lime pie where Miranda is from," Mr. Taylor said. "Which is . . . ?"

"Illinois," I finished.

"Ah," he said. "Illinois. Right."

"Have you been there?" I asked.

He shook his head as I followed him into the living room. Caleb, still looking glum, headed for the library. "It's hard to sail to Illinois."

"Oh yeah," I said. "No oceans. Well, there are some lakes. But mostly just corn. And more corn."

"I'm sure it's nice in its own way," Mr. Taylor said. "Most places are. Do *you* like it there?"

"Yeah," I said. "It's home."

"How did you end up on August Isle this summer? You said your mom had some important job to do?"

"She's a photographer," I explained. "She travels all around, kind of like you did, I guess. She's in Argentina right now. And my dad is working on this big legal case. So they sent me to stay with Sammy and Aunt Clare for the summer."

He furrowed his brow. "Aunt Clare?"

"Sammy's mom," I said. "She's not really my aunt. I don't have any aunts or uncles. I only have one set of grandparents, and my grandma just had hip surgery. So there wasn't anybody else. Aunt Clare is my mom's friend from when she was a kid. She used to come here in the summers, too."

"I see," said Mr. Taylor, settling on the couch and leaning down to wipe a scuff mark from his wooden clog. "Well, I hope you like it here."

"*You* must not have liked it much," I said, "since you went away for so long. People thought you were dead, you know."

A gray fog seemed to roll into his eyes. "You can love a place and still need to leave it behind for a while," he said. "Sometimes you have to leave or you'll go crazy."

"Yeah," I said. Before I could stop myself, I added, "I think that's how my mom feels sometimes."

A deep frown settled on his face. "I'm sure she just travels because it's her job. She probably misses you all the time. She's probably missing you right now."

"Maybe," I said flatly.

I could feel Mr. Taylor's gaze still on me, and I was relieved when Slug trotted back in, skittering on the hardwood floor, followed by Sammy.

"So," she said, "where do we start?"

We had the same duties as the day before. Caleb sat by a growing stack of books, some of them small and old, like the first edition of some Italian poetry book Mr. Taylor had found in a bookstall in Paris, and some big and new, like a collection of prints from the Mori Art Museum in Japan.

Sammy worked faster and faster on sorting pictures into albums as the stack of photos grew taller and taller. She only stopped every once in a while to ask Mr. Taylor about a particularly interesting one.

And I sat with his old laptop on my knees, my

fingers hovering over the keys, waiting for the next story.

In Finland, it is common for people to have summer cabins in the countryside. I once rented such a cabin—a mökki—on a very small island in a very big lake.

In the mornings, I rowed my boat around the lake. My favorite place to row to was a little cove in the shadow of a steep cliff. From there, I followed a trail that wove between the pine trees and around to the top of the cliff. Here, I would sit and eat my lunch and look out over the lake with its countless tiny islands.

One morning, I arrived to find a man diving in the deep water of the cove. "Ahoy there," I said. "Have you lost something?"

The man lifted his mask and stared at me, and I saw that he was actually a she. For a moment, I wasn't sure if she spoke English. "I haven't lost anything," she said finally. "But I am hoping to find something."

"Oh?" I asked. "What's that?"

Her gaze traveled from me down to the picnic I had prepared. "If you're willing to share," she said, "I'll tell you."

A few minutes later, we sat in the dappled

sun at the top of the cliff and nibbled at our rice porridge pastries and blueberries.

"There is a story around these parts," said the diver, "of a woman called Inkeri, who lived here many years ago. She was the eldest daughter of a rich landowner and known for her great beauty, but also her pure heart. Suitors came from miles around to seek Inkeri's hand in marriage, but she refused them all. She was already in love, you see, with one of the peasants who worked her father's farm, and they had determined to elope.

"But they were betrayed to Inkeri's father by another farmworker. When he found out about their plot, her father sent Inkeri's fiancé away to fight in a distant war. Then he set about finding her a new fiancé, someone rich and respectable like him. Every day, Inkeri came to this very spot to pray that her true love would return and take her away before her father succeeded.

"But her prayers went unanswered, for one day a letter arrived, announcing her beloved's death on the battlefield. Heartbroken, Inkeri wrote a note to her mother and sisters, telling them that she would rather join her betrothed in death than live and be married to someone she would never love. She called for her sleigh to be

prepared, and she drove it straight here. Only this time, instead of stopping to pray, she drove the sleigh over the cliff and into the lake below, which had not yet frozen over.

"At least," said the diver, glancing wryly at me, "that is one story. But one of Inkeri's sisters was not convinced. She believed that Inkeri jumped from the sleigh at the last second, faking her own death before escaping far away, somewhere her father could no longer control her fate."

"So you're looking for remnants of her sleigh?" I asked.

"Inkeri was my aunt many generations removed," said the woman. "Around here, people speak of her as 'poor, heartbroken Inkeri.' It is up to me to prove Inkeri's sister right, to search for proof of Inkeri's courage and cunning. Proof that behind her beauty, there was great strength. If I find a sleigh, but no skeleton, then I will know. Now I have told you why I am here. But why are you?"

After a few more moments, we had finished our picnic, and I could see that Inkeri's niece was eager to get back to her search. I wished her good luck and returned to my boat.

A few mornings later, I opened my door to

find a leather strap studded with bells that had been rusted silent. Attached to it was a note.

"Use this when you tell Inkeri's story. It's from the sleigh I recovered yesterday. There was no sign of Inkeri's remains. It seems appearances can be deceiving."

21

We *sat in silence* for a moment after Mr. Taylor finished speaking and I finished typing. Then he passed the strap to me, its bells rusted silent. I stroked the rough leather before handing it off to Sammy.

"I knew the woman was right," Sammy said. "I knew Inkeri ran away."

"Yeah, but I don't think she was right about Inkeri being very courageous," I said.

Mr. Taylor looked at me curiously. "Why's that?"

"Well, what about her family?" I asked, my hands clenching. "Her little sisters and her mom. She just left them behind. They probably really missed her. They probably relied on her for a lot."

"What was she supposed to do?" Caleb said. His

voice was tight, like a rubber band being snapped. "Marry some guy she didn't love? They would have been miserable together. She was better off running."

I had never seen Caleb get so worked up about anything. Sammy's jaw hung open, and she looked back and forth from me to Caleb. "What's your problem today?" she asked.

"It's not a problem to disagree," Mr. Taylor said, clearing his throat. "Stories change depending on who's listening to them. That's the beauty of them. Now I think it's time for Miranda to taste her first key lime pie."

A minute later, when Betsy bustled in from the kitchen, my hands unclenched, and I felt silly for caring so much about some old story.

"Best key lime pie in the state of Florida," Betsy crowed. "My grandmother's recipe. Always wins the August Festival pie contest."

"Miranda's entering that!" Sammy exclaimed.

"Are you, now?" Betsy asked.

"I don't know," I said quickly. "I'm not very good."

"Well you've certainly got *humble* pie down," she replied with a wink. "I'm sure you're better than you think."

Betsy's pie *was* really good. Smooth, tart, and sweet. I gobbled down my first slice, then asked for another.

"Aha!" Betsy exclaimed. "Another convert. Mama will be delighted to know."

"Does she live here, too?" Sammy asked.

"Mama's spent her whole life on this island," Betsy said. "All ninety-nine years of it."

"Your mom is *ninety-nine*?" Caleb asked.

"That's right," she said. "It's the pie. It keeps her young."

When we were finished for the afternoon, Mr. Taylor walked Sammy and Caleb out, but I stole past the dining room and toward the swinging kitchen door.

"Betsy?" I called.

She suddenly appeared, filling the doorway, pushing me back out into the living room. "Kitchen's a mess," she said, blowing a curl back from her face. "I can't allow any guest to see it that way."

"Oh," I said. "That's okay. I just wondered—"

"Yes, dear?"

"Well, your pie was so good," I said. "And I tried to make one last night, but the crust didn't come out right. So I guess I just wondered if you had any, like, tips?"

"Hmmm," Betsy hummed, tapping her nail to her lip. "Well, how were you feeling last night?"

"What?" I asked.

"Were you distracted? Upset or anxious about anything?"

I *had* gotten Mom's text right before we started baking. "Maybe a little distracted."

"There's your problem," she said. "You can't make

a piecrust when you're upset or distracted. No matter what you do, the dough just won't cooperate. Next time, you have to block everything else out. Treat the dough like it's the only thing in life that matters. *That's* how you make a good piecrust."

"Okay," I said. "Thanks a lot."

"No problem," Betsy said. "I could use a little competition."

She winked and disappeared back into the kitchen.

I waved goodbye to Mr. Taylor and skipped out to join Sammy and Caleb, who were waiting on the sidewalk.

"Man, is that guy lucky," Caleb said.

"What do you mean?" Sammy asked.

"Come on. Sailing around the globe? Just going wherever the wind blows you, not a problem in the world? Sounds like a pretty good life to me."

"I don't know," I said slowly, thinking about what Mr. Taylor had told me about needing to get away from August Isle. "When he was talking to me, it kind of sounded like he didn't really *want* to leave, but he had to."

"What do you mean?" Sammy asked, looking up into the sun and squinting.

"I'm not really sure."

"Well, he's got a story all right," Sammy said. "One that he won't tell us. The question is . . . why?"

22

By the next day, Caleb was back to normal again. I think he might have even felt kind of bad for snapping at me at Mr. Taylor's. During our sailing lesson, Jason had us take turns using the tiller and sail to steer our boats through a little obstacle course he'd made with buoys (still where the water was shallow enough that I knew I would be able to touch the sandy bottom if I fell out).

"Hey, nice job," Caleb said once I had finished. He leaned over the side of his boat to give me a high five as I skimmed by.

"Thanks," I replied, cheeks flushing with pride.

And after our lesson, he stuck around, tagging along as we went to check on the sea turtle's nest (still there, still kind of boring) and get ice cream (goat cheese for Caleb, pineapple for me, and chili chocolate for Sammy) to eat under the August Oak.

I got the feeling that Sammy and Caleb mostly liked sitting there because it was in the shade, and because all the rustling leaves made a little breeze that kept the heat from being so bad. But I loved it because being inside the bell of its branches somehow made me feel safe and cozy, kind of the way I felt back in Illinois when it was snowing outside and I was curled up on the couch with a mug of hot chocolate.

When it was time to go to Mr. Taylor's, Caleb showed us a shortcut. His dad was a vacation rental agent, he told us, which meant he had memorized pretty much every street on the Isle.

I was still thinking about the high five Caleb had given me that morning when my toes caught on something and suddenly I felt myself lunge forward. Before I could fall, though, hands gripped me on either side.

"Thanks," I muttered as Caleb and Sammy steadied me.

"No biggie," Caleb said. "Everyone trips there."

I looked down to see that a square of sidewalk had been pushed up by one of the August Oak's reaching roots.

Sammy linked her arm through mine. "Here," she said. "Now it's impossible for you to trip."

Still, I kept my eyes on my feet as we left Oak Street behind. Anyone could have tripped on that bit of sidewalk—Caleb had said so himself. But only a true klutz would trip twice in ten minutes.

It had started to rain, and as I watched, the sidewalk began to freckle with little droplets. Then I noticed something else up ahead.

Words that had been written into the concrete when it was still wet.

Names. Three of them, each written in a different handwriting, stacked one on top of another.

Clare

Beth

Ben

A nearby peal of thunder shook my stomach. It had begun to rain harder. Sammy pulled her arm away and began to run, but I didn't move. I had to squat down to get a better look. I traced my mother's name with my own finger. She still wrote her B's with the same big swoops.

I had pretty much given up on my investigation after Aunt Clare showed me those photos of Mom. I wasn't sure I could handle finding out anything more about her past.

But now I was staring at a clue. I was *standing* on it.

"Miranda!" Sammy was calling. "Come on! We're getting wet."

When I didn't come, Sammy jogged back to me. "What's up?"

I pointed at the sidewalk.

"'Clare, Beth, Ben,'" she read. "Hey, that's cool! But who's Ben?"

"You don't know?"

Sammy shook her head. "All I know is we're going to get soaked if we stay here. Let's go!"

I took one last look at the names, a weird feeling stirring in my chest that I didn't have a name for. Then I tore my gaze away and ran after Sammy and Caleb.

Once we got to Mr. Taylor's, I didn't have much time to think about the names, because he put us straight to work. Our first crate that day was from Sweden, and the first thing I pulled out of it was a small black box.

Inside was a dainty necklace. After I booted up the old laptop, Mr. Taylor flipped to a new page in his notebook and began to read.

Stockholm in the winter was like a great swan resting on the edge of the sea, with feathers so white, they sparkled. One snowy evening there, I was eating a late supper in a restaurant and watching the passersby, huddled in their parkas and wool scarves, when a man came out from the kitchen.

He greeted me and asked me how my food was, and I soon realized that he was the owner. His accent was not Swedish, and he walked with a slight limp. Flecks of gold swam in the deep shadows of his eyes. Too deep for a man so young. I asked if he might sit a moment with a stranger and tell me his story.

"My story is the story of my country," he said, "and what happened when it fell apart. It starts when I was only a boy, and trouble had been brewing for many months. Later, people would call it the Bosnian War, but back then it was simply a storm darkening the ridge of the mountains that guarded our village. My family had lived there all our lives, in a cottage where I shared a room with my three sisters.

"We had greater things to worry about than war. My father owned a small shop, and we never seemed to have enough food or fuel. Sometimes I would become angry at the way we lived, especially when I went with my mother to the nearest town to sell the plums and sloeberries she grew in the summer. There, everyone seemed to own a TV, and shoes that had no holes. My anger hurt my parents deeply, because they

believed there was honor in working hard and being honest people.

"One spring day, when the whispers of war had grown too loud to ignore, my mother and I went to town. People kept their heads down, and everyone seemed to be in a hurry. As we walked, I saw a man beside me drop something, and when I bent down to pick it up, I saw that it was a large bill.

"I nearly called out to the man, but my voice caught in my throat. I thought of the things I could buy with such money. A good soccer ball, or all the candy I could carry, or maybe even a new pair of shoes. I quickly shoved the bill into my pocket. It weighed almost nothing, yet it felt heavy in my coat. Almost immediately, I wished I could give it back, but the man who had dropped it had already disappeared.

"I decided I could not spend the money on myself but would instead buy something beautiful for my mother. I settled on a delicate copper necklace with a tiny turquoise pendant. But when I gave the necklace to her that night— telling her I had found it on the street—she began to cry. She pushed the gift back into my hands, telling me to return it. She knew I could not have come by it honestly. I had never felt a

guilt so great, like a whale in my belly.

"Only a week later, war came to our village and my father was killed trying to defend his shop. The rest of us fled through the woods. We settled for a while in a new town, but then the shelling started, and our flat caught fire. My mother and one of my sisters did not make it out. My eldest sister took my little sister and me onward. She made us keep going, even when we had no food, even when the cold bit our fingers. Eventually we made it to safety and were resettled here, in Sweden.

"All the time, I carried the necklace in my pocket. I began to believe that it was cursed. Perhaps if I had been content in my life, if I had not stolen the money and bought the necklace, war would have missed our village. Perhaps my mother and father and sister would be alive, and we would be together always."

Then he dug into his pocket and pulled out the little necklace. It dangled from his palm.

"Surely you didn't actually believe that," I said. "Stealing that money didn't cause any of those things."

"I know that now," said the man, "but back then, I felt that at least if I caused these terrible things to happen, it meant I had some power

over what had been done to me. Better to be guilty than powerless, yes?"

He dropped the necklace into my palm and closed my fingers around it. "You take it," he said. "I have held it for far too long. Now tell me, friend, what weight do you carry in your pocket?"

23

Between spending our mornings at sailing lessons and our afternoons at Mr. Taylor's house, the days began to feel like the roller coaster that Sammy, Caleb, and I rode the next time we went to the park.

At first, summer had passed so slowly, like our car inching up the tracks while I gripped Sammy's hand tight with fear. But then suddenly the days were zooming by, faster and faster, until one afternoon I realized that my month on August Isle was halfway over.

And somewhere along the way, I had come to love it there.

I loved the way my skin always smelled like sunscreen and my hair tasted like salt.

I loved how it felt to stand in the surf and let my ankles sink into the sand, and to sit in the dappled light under the August Oak as Sammy, Caleb, and I licked our way through every flavor at Sundae's.

I loved how every morning, my heart beat hard as Jason and I sailed a little farther from shore than we had the day before. And how, when the lesson was over and we were sailing back to shore again, a lantern of pride would burn bright in my heart.

I even loved the feeling of sand at the foot of my bed every night, like a little bit of the beach had followed me home.

More than anything, though, I loved going to Mr. Taylor's house.

The rest of the Isle—the beach, the harbor, even the August Oak—was for everyone. But Mr. Taylor's house seemed to exist just for him and Betsy and us. No one else ever came to or went from it, although once or twice we did see the round face of the lady next door peering through her window as we arrived.

And then there were the stories.

The stories were what made my heart start to flutter as we set out for Mr. Taylor's house every day, and what always made us run the last few blocks to reach it.

You could almost hear them as the house came into view, buzzing inside like a colony of bees. We heard the hum of them in our bones, even if we didn't always understand exactly what they meant.

There was the Bosnian refugee who had blamed himself for his family's tragedy, and the hermit who lived up in the Ethiopian highlands, whittling exquisite birdhouses that no one had ever seen. There was the lonely Chinese woman who received a message in a bottle from her dead husband, sixty-three years after it was sent, and the Siberian boy who really had spent a year being raised by wolves.

We always discussed the stories afterward, either with Mr. Taylor or on our own once we'd left his house. Had the Bosnian man ever forgiven himself for a war that was not his fault? What was the point of carving beautiful houses if only birds could see them?

Every time we passed the sea turtle's nest, I would think of what Sammy had said about how most of the hatchlings would die, and then I'd remember the words of the Dutch tulip farmer: *Often the most exquisite things are the first to fade away. And life is the most exquisite thing of all.*

I thought I at least understood what that story meant—that life was fragile and short, but maybe knowing this helped us appreciate it more.

Every afternoon, we pleaded with Mr. Taylor to tell us *his* story. But each time, he shook his head and said, "Not today." Then he called for Betsy to bring out whatever she had baked for us.

* * *

Not every object we unpacked from the boxes came with a story. Some of their stories had already been forgotten. There was the blue South African butterfly pinned behind a sheet of glass that Mr. Taylor thought might be the last specimen of its species. The Swiss music box he'd found in an antique shop that played a haunting melody none of us had ever heard. There were maps of countries that no longer existed, books of legends no one had told for centuries, and portraits of people whose names no one could remember.

At least they wouldn't disappear completely now.

Mr. Taylor started letting Safira out of her cage when we came. She would stand on a perch by the window, looking out and cawing in Portuguese at passersby, or hop over to the arm of the couch to settle by Mr. Taylor as we worked. He stroked her downy head and fed her macadamia nuts from a bowl on the table that was always full.

Once, Sammy brought a bit of rope we'd found on the beach. She tried to tempt Slug into playing tug-of-war, but he merely glared at it for a moment before falling asleep again.

"Try Safira," Mr. Taylor said.

"Really?" Sammy asked, looking worriedly at the parrot's beak, nearly as big as my hand.

Before he could answer, Safira had descended from

her perch and begun to pull at the rope, first with her talons and then with her beak, twisting her head and sticking out her black tongue. I decided Mr. Taylor must have been teasing Caleb on our first day when he told him to be careful of his fingers, because Safira was very gentle.

Sometimes, when Caleb went to take an armload of books to the library, he would take her, too, and we would hear him trying to teach her to say something in English, but she stuck stubbornly with her few words of Portuguese. And even though she still screeched "Ladrão!" every time we came—which Mr. Taylor said meant robber—I didn't think she really meant it. It was just her way of saying hello.

I looked forward to the evenings at Sammy's house almost as much as I did the afternoons at Mr. Taylor's.

The day after we made our peach cobbler, Aunt Clare went out and bought me an apron of my own, green with red hibiscus flowers, and a blue-and-white pie dish she said would both be mine to keep at the end of the summer.

Every night since, we had tried a new kind of pie together. First cherry, then strawberry, and then chocolate chess. Sometimes Sammy helped, too, but other times she just DJed from her laptop, playing her favorite pop songs, both Indian and American. Meanwhile,

Jai taught Caleb—who followed us home pretty much every night—different chords on his guitar.

Before I started to mix the dough for the piecrust, I always remembered Betsy's advice. I took a deep breath and tried to push everything—especially Mom—from my head. If I let myself start thinking about her, I would start to wonder what she was doing at that very moment, and if she missed me at all, and when she was going to call again.

At first, I was really nervous about letting everyone try our pies. They never came out just right—the crust was too thick or the filling too runny. But then I reminded myself that I wasn't just supposed to be brave now. I was supposed to be *bold*, too.

Brave was sailing farther away from shore every morning, and keeping my eyes open on the roller coaster as we plummeted toward the ground.

But bold was something different. Bold meant not always trying to blend into the background. It meant that sometimes you had to stand out, even when you didn't know what people would think of you. Like sharing the pies I had worked hard on even though they might not be very good, or entering a big contest even though I probably wouldn't win.

And anyway, Uncle Amar always swore our newest attempt was the best pie he had ever tasted. Aunt Clare never seemed to mind that the kitchen looked like a disaster zone when we were done, either.

Sometimes I remembered what I had overheard them say the night after our first sailing lesson. Maybe they still thought I was a burden, and they were just doing a really good job of hiding it. But I had started to convince myself that I was changing the way they thought of me. Which meant maybe I really could change the way Mom saw me, too.

"Thanks for helping me so much, Aunt Clare," I said one night, as we were sponging flour off the counters. "It's really nice of you."

"Are you kidding?" she said. "You're helping *me*! I never would have learned to make a pie if you hadn't come to stay. Maybe now I'll finally be allowed back into my mother-in-law's kitchen! I'm still not sure we've found the right pie for the festival, though. We need to think of something really special."

I nodded. A question hovered on my lips.

I hadn't forgotten the names in the sidewalk. Especially Ben. Every day, I thought about asking Aunt Clare who he was, but every time I came close, I remembered how much it hurt to see those photos of Mom. And even though the brave thing to do would be to ask the question, I swallowed it down instead.

"Everything okay?" Aunt Clare asked.

I didn't say anything. Instead I flung my arms around her. She gave a surprised laugh as she looped her arms around my back. "I'm so glad you came this summer, Miranda," she said. "You're a good kid."

To my surprise, she kissed the top of my head. And when she pulled away, she wore a sad little smile. A bittersweet-chocolate smile.

One morning, *Jason and* I watched from our boat as Sammy and Caleb practiced capsizing theirs. The two of them stood together on one side of the boat and wrapped their hands around the mast until the hull keeled over and they fell, laughing, into the water.

I felt a tiny pang of jealousy as Caleb gave Sammy a boost up to reach the daggerboard—this little plastic wedge that cut through the bottom of the boat. She grabbed it and pulled the boat sideways, then climbed up to stand on the daggerboard and tugged the boat the rest of the way up.

Jason whistled through his fingers. "Great job, guys!" he called. Then he turned to me. "Sure you don't want to try?"

I hooked my fingers through the flaps of my life jacket. We were already deeper in the harbor than we had ever gone before. Definitely too deep to touch. On the boat, I could avoid thinking about that if I kept myself busy. But in the water, I knew, my toes would thrash to find the bottom, and when they couldn't, I would start to panic.

"I don't think I'm ready," I said. "Not yet."

"That's okay," Jason said. "You're doing great, Miranda. Really. You've got a knack for this."

He probably had to say that, since he was my sailing instructor and all, but it felt good to hear anyway.

As I turned my gaze back to Sammy and Caleb, my eye caught something rippling through the water.

I gasped. There was a dark shape down there, gliding along beneath us. I clutched at Jason's wrist.

"What is that?" I asked, jabbing my finger toward the thing.

He looked down at the water. "Sammy, Caleb!" he called. "Come here! There's a sea turtle!"

"A—sea turtle?" I asked, letting go of Jason and peering over the side. Wasn't the thing below us too big to be a turtle? It was almost as wide as our little boat.

But then a leathery head popped up to the surface, just long enough for me to see the turtle's solemn teardrop eyes and the way its skin was chocolaty brown, latticed with narrow ribbons of white. I gasped.

"It's so—" I started. For a minute, I couldn't find the right word. Beautiful wasn't quite it, and neither was magic. Then I remembered. "August. It's so august."

The turtle was already off again, gliding through the water toward Caleb and Sammy, who dove down together to swim alongside it for a few strokes.

I felt another squeeze of jealousy. Because of the sea turtle.

Mostly because of the sea turtle.

"Sure is," Jason said. "That was a big one."

"Maybe she's the one who made the nest on the beach!" I said. I knew it probably wasn't true, but it made me feel happy to imagine that the turtle mother might be biding her time, waiting for her eggs to hatch so she could guide the babies to safety.

Just then, Caleb surfaced next to our boat. "Look what I found," he said, flopping something orange down beside me. "I, um, thought you might like to see it."

I felt a spark of delight as I realized it was a starfish. When I picked it up, it was soft and squishy.

"It's still alive," Jason explained, "so be careful."

"Oh, wow!" I breathed, watching wide-eyed as it wrapped one of its little legs around my finger. I had a tugging feeling that it reminded me of something, but I couldn't think of what. "Thanks!"

I held it for a minute, wondering what life was like as a starfish, then passed it back to Caleb, who dropped it gently into the sea.

That afternoon, while Sammy and Caleb were feeding Safira macadamia nuts, Mr. Taylor asked me how I was enjoying my stay on August Isle.

"I love it here."

Mr. Taylor smiled. "That's good," he said. "Not too homesick?"

"No," I said honestly.

"Do you hear much from your mom?" His eyes rounded with pity in the corners, and I wished I hadn't ever blurted out anything about Mom to Mr. Taylor. These afternoons belonged to Sammy and Caleb and me. I didn't want to share them with Mom.

I hadn't thought much about her at all that day. And not thinking about her had made me feel lighter somehow.

"She texts me sometimes," I said. To be exact, she had texted me three times and called me once since sending me the mountain picture. The line was all funny and echoey when she called, though, so we hadn't talked for long. "She doesn't have a lot of cell service. But my dad calls me a lot."

"I see," said Mr. Taylor, one corner of his beard twitching.

"We saw a sea turtle today," I said, to change the subject. "It was huge."

"Oh, yes?" Mr. Taylor said, blinking. When he opened his eyes again, the pity in them was gone, and I breathed a sigh of relief. "They're amazing creatures, aren't they?"

"Yeah," said Sammy, drifting over. "Caleb and I swam beside it for a while. It was so cool!"

"But not you, Miranda?" Mr. Taylor asked.

"She's scared of the water," Caleb said, still stroking Safira.

"Caleb!" Sammy clucked.

"It's okay," I said. "It's true. I am scared of water."

"Are you, now?" Little thought lines appeared between Mr. Taylor's bushy eyebrows. "Well, that's nothing to be ashamed of. Everyone is scared of something."

"Like my fear of Swiss cheese," Sammy said, giggling.

"That's a stupid fear," Caleb said.

She scowled. "Is not. All those holes are disgusting. Anyway, what are *you* afraid of? It's probably even weirder."

For a second, Caleb's face seemed to crumple. Then it was back to normal, like an umbrella that had been turned inside out by the wind and then back again. "I'm not afraid of anything."

Sammy opened her mouth to argue, but I touched her arm and gave a slight shake of my head.

"Anyway," I said, "I'm trying not to be so scared anymore."

"Ah," Mr. Taylor said. "Well now, there I think I may be able to help."

Then he cast his eyes over the remaining crates. I saw, with a sad squeeze of my stomach, that they were over halfway gone. He pointed to one at the bottom of a stack. "Try that box there. Could you bring it over, Caleb?"

Caleb heaved the two top boxes to the side and then pushed the bottom one across the ruby-and-sapphire rug. Mr. Taylor leaned down and opened the lid, pulling out a small object wrapped in newspaper and tied with twine.

He unwrapped the newspaper to reveal a silver dagger, its blade slightly rusted, its handle inky black.

When Caleb saw it, he stopped dead. "Whoa," he breathed. "What's that for?"

25

I once stayed for a month in a small town in the foothills of the Himalayas. Every morning, I went to the one café in town, and every morning, I had the same waitress, a young woman with kindness in her eyes.

One day, when I had been there a few weeks, we began to talk, and I realized that she spoke quite good English. It had grown rusty from disuse, she said. "So has my voice," I told her, for I had not had a real conversation with anyone since I arrived.

From that morning on, I came to the café early, before it officially opened, and while she *prepared for the day, the young woman and I would have long conversations. When I told her that I was a collector of stories, she hesitated for a moment, then nodded in silent decision.*

"You will come," she said, "and eat with my family. My grandmother, she has many stories that should be remembered when she is gone. She is very sick already and has not much time."

The next night, I found myself in her home, surrounded by her family and the feast they had cooked for me. When we were done with our beef dumplings and noodle soup and butter tea, she led me to the room where her grandmother lay. With the young woman's help, her grandmother sat up and began to speak a language I did not understand. Her granddaughter translated her words for me.

The grandmother wanted to know what questions I had for her. I thought for a moment, then asked if she was afraid to die. She considered my question and then, to my surprise, pulled something out from under her narrow mattress. I saw that she was holding a small knife with a black handle.

"When my father was a young boy," the old woman said, "he lived in a nearby village surrounded by a dark forest. Most of the boys in his

village did not go to school, but instead helped their fathers with their farms and livestock. But my grandmother insisted that my father should get an education, so every day he walked miles through the forest to get to school and back.

"One winter, yaks began to go missing from the farms. The farmers whispered that some fearsome beast was attacking them and dragging them into the forest, where it would feast on its prey. One brave farmer strode into the forest with a machete, determined to kill the beast. But he never returned.

"My father grew very afraid, but my grandmother insisted that he carry on going to school. So my grandfather fashioned a dagger, which he gave to my father for protection. Every morning and every afternoon, my father clutched the dagger tightly inside his warm pocket as he walked.

"Soon my father began to feel that something was following him. He felt hungry eyes upon him. But whenever he looked over his shoulder, nothing was there. Still, his heart pounded with fear every time he stepped into the trees.

"Then one day, my father heard the snapping of a twig not far in front of him. He raised his dagger in fear that it was the beast, but instead two men stepped into view. Before he could say *anything, the men cried out and pointed over his shoulder. My father turned to see a huge snow leopard, its fur bristling and its mouth curled into a ferocious snarl, standing at his heels.*

"My father knew at once that this leopard had been the thing that had stalked him for weeks. He knew he was staring his own death in the face. But when the leopard moved, it leaped past my father and pounced on the first of the two men, who let out a horrible cry and then went silent. The other man lifted a machete and swung it at the leopard, but before he could strike his mark, the beast had grabbed his thigh in its jaws and dragged him to the ground.

"Stunned, my father remained frozen, dagger still raised in his fist. When the leopard had finished with the two men, it looked back at him. Their gaze met for a moment in the snowy forest, and then the leopard brushed past him, flicking its tail gently against his belly, and disappeared into the trees.

"My father went to the fallen men to see if either was still alive. It was only then, standing over their bodies, that he recognized the coat around the shoulders of the second man. It belonged to the farmer who had gone bravely into the forest. My father was standing over two

dead bandits, who had stolen livestock from the village and killed the farmer who had stumbled upon them. They would surely have killed my father, too.

"He realized then that the snow leopard had been following him all those weeks to protect him from these evil men. The thing he had most feared was the very thing that had saved him. He saw then how his fear had blinded him to the true nature of the thing he was afraid of."

The old woman turned away from the past and looked at me with her clouded eyes. "As a young girl, I was scared of death," she said. "But now I wait to embrace him as I would a loyal friend. So I have no need for this any longer." She slowly handed me the dagger and closed my fingers around it. "Now tell me, young man, what is it you fear?"

The next day, as we sailed out into the harbor, I remembered what the old woman in the story had said about fear.

And I thought that maybe there were different kinds of fear. There was a good kind of fear that made you careful. The kind that kept you on your guard when walking through a dark forest, or that made you remember to wear your life jacket on the water.

And then there was the kind that held you back. The kind that kept you from going to school and had kept me frozen on the beach that first lesson. If you let that kind of fear take over, you could stay frozen forever—never changing, never growing. Never feeling the wind on your face or leaning down to let the water rush between your fingers as you skimmed over the waves.

So I pulled the sail tight against the wind and imagined the turtle we had seen the day before keeping close by, ready to save me if I fell into the water.

I thought about Sammy telling me to remember all the good things about the ocean, like the seahorses and the dolphins and the rainbow coral reefs Mr. Taylor had seen on his travels.

And I remembered how at night, the surf sounded like a lullaby rocking me to sleep.

I took a deep breath. "I think we can go farther out today," I said to Jason.

"Oh yeah?"

"Yeah."

"Think you'll be ready to sail past the harbor soon?"

I stared at the mouth of the harbor. Beyond it, the ocean stretched on forever.

"Yeah," I said. "Soon."

26

As the end of my third week on August Isle hurtled nearer, I started to notice a sickly feeling in the pit of my stomach. Every day, as the number of boxes at Mr. Taylor's house dwindled, the feeling got a little bit bigger, like the thunder that comes as a storm draws closer and closer.

I felt it most during quiet moments, like when we were all sitting around after dessert at Sammy's table, too stuffed to talk anymore.

And I felt it at the end of that week as Caleb, Sammy, and I walked to Sundae's before heading to Mr. Taylor's for the afternoon. It was so hot that it was hard to catch my breath, and the drone of the cicadas in the August Oak made me feel drowsy as we passed underneath its limbs. Everything felt slow, like the tails of Spanish moss swaying back and forth in the breeze.

But time is going by fast, I reminded myself. *And there aren't many days left now.*

The sickly feeling crept closer. I must have looked sick, too, because Sammy stopped and turned to me as we reached Sundae's. "What's wrong?"

"Nothing," I replied. "Except, well, I was just thinking how much I was going to miss all this."

"All what?" Caleb asked.

"Well, you guys, for one," I said, stealing a glance at him. Had he thought at all about missing me when I was gone?

"Nothing will be the same after you leave," Sammy said, sighing.

"True," Caleb said. "Who will we break into old people's houses with? And who's going to make us pie every night?"

Out of the corner of my eye, I saw Sammy elbow him.

"Ow! I'm just kidding," he said. "This summer started off pretty bad, but it turned out okay. It kind of sucks that you have to leave. You'll come back, though, right?"

I wondered what he meant about the summer

starting off bad, but only for a second. More important, Caleb wanted me to come back.

"You will," Sammy said firmly. "You and your mom
both."

Sammy didn't know about the postcards, or about
how Mom never seemed to want to talk about the Isle.
I hadn't thought much about those things either, I
realized, since my first week there. I didn't argue with
her, though. "You can always visit me in Illinois, too,"
I said instead.

Sammy flashed her braces, looped her arm around
my waist, and ordered Caleb to open the door. We
squeezed through, each of us bumping our shoulder
on the doorframe.

"This must be what it feels like to be Slug," I said.
Sammy giggled.

Inside, she ordered a double cone of the daily flavor, raspberry lemonade. Caleb asked for honeysuckle,
and I got sugarplum. When Sammy took her first lick,
she closed her eyes in a blissful expression. "You have
to try this," she said. "I think it might be my all-time
favorite."

We swapped cones and I tasted hers. She was
right—it was amazing. Sour enough to make your lips
pucker, but sweet enough that you didn't mind. "Why
didn't I order this?" I asked. "They won't have it next
time we come."

"I want to eat this every day," Sammy groaned, reluctantly handing the cone over to Caleb to try.

"Hey!" I said suddenly. "What if I could make a pie that tasted like this? A raspberry-lemonade pie?"

"Then I would love you forever," Sammy said. "Do you think you can?"

"Maybe."

Aunt Clare had said we would need something special for the contest. Maybe that meant making up my own recipe. As we left the shop, my mind began running through lists of possible ingredients, which was a good distraction from thinking about how much I would miss the Isle.

I didn't even notice that we had taken Caleb's shortcut again. Not until Sammy stopped and pointed at her feet.

"Hey," she said, "we totally forgot about this!"

"Oh yeah," I mumbled, looking down at the names written in the sidewalk. Even though I hadn't forgotten at all.

"Who are these people?" Caleb asked.

"Well, Clare is my mom, duh, and Beth is Miranda's mom, and Ben is a mystery. We should ask my mom."

"He was probably just a random friend," I said.

"Yeah, probably," Sammy replied, shrugging. "Mom said they had tons."

As we walked the rest of the way to Mr. Taylor's, though, I couldn't stop thinking about Ben. And Mom.

When I came to the Isle, I thought I might find some kind of clue about why everything had changed between Mom and me. Since I'd never been able to find one at home, August Isle seemed like as good a place as any to look.

Then Aunt Clare showed me those pictures, and I overheard her and Uncle Amar talking about me, and suddenly I understood why things between Mom and me had changed. It had nothing to do with the Isle and everything to do with me.

But I still didn't have an answer to any of the other questions I started with. The ones Sammy had reminded me of when she'd said that Mom would come back to the Isle someday. Why *did* Mom always throw away Aunt Clare's postcards? Why *wouldn't* she ever talk about the Isle? And if she had been so happy here, why had she ever stopped coming in the first place?

Now the questions began to bother me again, like bits of flaking sunburn I really wanted to peel. They had replaced all thoughts of pie by the time we arrived at Mr. Taylor's and followed him into the living room.

"You seem distracted today," Mr. Taylor said, frowning from across the sofa as we sat down.

"Sorry," I said. "I kind of have a lot on my mind."

"Ah," he breathed. "Caleb, would you take that stack of books into my library? It's leaning like the Tower of Pisa. Sammy, perhaps you could help him. Some of those titles are quite valuable. They need clean hands."

The creases in his brow doubled as he stared at the dribble of dried ice cream on Caleb's chin.

When Sammy and Caleb had each taken half the stack of books and disappeared into the library ("Ladrão! Polícia!" squawked Safira, who had been dozing in her cage), Mr. Taylor cleared his throat.

"Penny for your thoughts," he said. "Though really, they should change the expression. It was coined—pardon the pun—back when a penny was quite a large sum of money. Thoughts are valuable things, you know. They shouldn't be ignored. Especially the ones that trouble you."

I bit my lip. How much should I say? Hadn't I already told Mr. Taylor too much about Mom? The last thing I wanted was him feeling sorry for me again.

"Just family stuff," I said.

"Your mother?"

I hesitated, then nodded. He had already guessed it anyway.

"I'm sorry. Family problems can be the hardest

ones to solve sometimes."

"Do you have a family?" I asked, my eyes glancing around the room I already knew held no family portraits, only cheerful paintings of the beach.

Mr. Taylor gazed out the window, and a smile wisped across his face. To me, it seemed like an echo of one that had touched his lips a long time ago. "Everyone has a family, Miranda."

"Right," I said. "It's just—you tell all these stories, but you never talk about yourself. So I didn't know if . . ."

"Well, I'm certainly no expert in this area," he said. The smile had faded now. "Ask me about tulip mania in the Dutch Golden Age or the migration patterns of the saddle-billed stork and I can talk all day. Families are far more complicated."

"Tell me about it."

A sigh rose up in his chest. "Here's what I *can* tell you," he said finally. "Because I'm old and I have met many families. And I know all of them have their problems. Every single one."

"Maybe," I said. "But some problems are bigger than others."

"Certainly," Mr. Taylor agreed. "But I don't think the merit of a family is in how large or small their problems are. It's in how they face those problems. To me, the most beautiful families are the ones who have the toughest trials and still find a way to help each other through."

He spoke slowly, like he was choosing each word very carefully. When he was done, we sat silently for a moment, listening to Sammy scolding Caleb for attempting to teach Safira a curse word.

"I'm trying to fix them," I said. "Our problems."

"Well, you can't do it on your own, can you? Your mom has to do her part, too."

"How do you know?" I asked. "That it's not just me? That *I'm* not the problem?"

"Because you're only a child," he said. "I know children don't like to hear that, but it's true. And children aren't responsible for adults' problems. Believe me, we adults do a fine job making problems for ourselves."

I knew he was trying to make me feel better, but somehow his words only made me more frustrated.

"Well, if I'm not responsible, what is?" I asked.

Mr. Taylor considered this for a moment, then pointed a finger out the window. "You see my gates?" he asked. I followed his gaze, staring at the low iron gates I had climbed over the night I broke in. "Do you see that symbol inside them?"

On each gate, at the center of the black bars, the metal had been bent to form two S's that came together with curls on each end.

"It's a fancy heart," I said.

"That's what I used to think, too," Mr. Taylor said. Then he stood and began to rummage through the remaining three boxes, until finally he pulled out a large gray cloth. "But then I found this."

27

The winds blew me to the west coast of Africa one fall, and I set my sails to rest for a time in Accra, the capital of Ghana. There I fell in love with the warmth of the people, the colors of the land, the movements of the bustling city.

One afternoon I ventured out to Makola Market, where vendors sold anything you can imagine to buy—miles of fruit, towering heaps of clothes, endless electronics. The air was filled with the sounds of haggling and honking horns and vendors selling their wares, as well as waves of smells—a rainbow of spices and rows of dried fish.

I was accompanied by a law student at a local university who was paying his way by giving tours. He led me through the tightly packed crowds to a fabric stall where he asked a woman to pull out several different cloths, each of them in solid colors with black symbols imprinted in small squares throughout.

"It's beautiful fabric," I said.

"Not only fabric," corrected my guide. "This is adinkra cloth. Every symbol on it represents a piece of wisdom passed down along many generations of Ashanti people. Our ancestors created these symbols so that we would not forget what they had learned."

I studied the cloth. "Don't you think some things would be easier to forget?"

My guide stared at me for a long moment, his eyebrows knitting together in disapproval.

"I grew up not far from here," he said to me, "in a beautiful house where I wanted for nothing. I had the best clothes, the best food, and the best schools. I had everything except the one thing I wanted most.

"No matter how well I did in school or sports, it never seemed good enough to win my father's approval. He always thought I could do better, work harder. And when it was time to go

to university, he refused to pay my tuition, although he could certainly have afforded it. He told me I would have to get a job and pay my own way.

"That night, my mother found me crying in my room. When she asked me what was wrong, I told her that I hated my father as he surely hated me. That I was no son of his.

"The next morning, my mother woke me early and told me to get dressed and meet her in our car. We drove northwest for hours until we came to a little town outside of Kumasi, where the houses were small and run-down. 'This,' she said, 'is where your father was raised. He is ashamed of this place. But there is no shame in where we are born. When I see this town, it reminds me how hard your father worked for a better life. Never slowing, never resting.'

"I could not believe my ears," said the young man. "I had no idea that my father had been poor. That it was only thanks to a kind teacher who saw his potential and an aunt who moved to Accra and found a scholarship for him that he ever left his town. And I understood then that he did not hate me. He was merely afraid. Afraid that he could still end up back where he had begun. Afraid that I might end up there, too, if

he did not teach me to be like him—never slowing, never resting. He did not want me to know the suffering he had known."

I placed my hand on his shoulder then, for though I did not know his father, I, too, had known a man like this once. "He loves you," I said, "in the best way he knows how."

The young man took the cloth from me then and pointed to a heartlike symbol. "This," he said, "is sankofa: the symbol for a proverb that says it is not wrong to go back and remember our past. In fact, to move forward, we must honor our history, and learn from it. Sankofa reminds us that it is always better to remember, even when remembering is the hardest thing to do. Perhaps especially then. Do you see?"

I looked down at the cloth he held, tracing the symbol with my mind's eye. Though it was a warm day, I felt a shiver pass through me. "Yes," I said. "I think perhaps I do."

"It wasn't until I arrived back home that I even noticed the sankofa on my own front gates," Mr. Taylor said. "You see, when west Africans were captured and brought here to be slaves, they brought their stories with them. Slave owners would try to stamp such stories out, to strip these captives of their humanity, but they found ways to remember who they really were. And to remind the generations that would follow that they were not slaves but people like any others—people with histories and families—who had been enslaved."

"Wow," I said. We had studied slavery in history class last year, but we didn't learn anything about sankofas or adinkra cloth. I wondered what else our textbook had left out. "It's like a secret message."

"It is indeed," agreed Mr. Taylor. "The same proverb is also symbolized sometimes by a bird that's looking backward. And I think if you look closely at the gates, the two sides of the heart look like two birds. The curls at the bottom are like feet, pointing forward. But the curls at the top are their heads, pointing backward, toward one another."

If I scrunched up my eyes, the two halves of the heart kind of did look like birds. "So they're moving forward, but looking back?" I asked.

"Exactly," Mr. Taylor said.

"And you're saying . . . I should be like those birds?"

"I suppose I'm saying that the past is often the best place to look when we need help understanding something in our present. If I were you, that's where I would start with trying to understand your mother."

But hadn't I already done that? Aunt Clare's photos had given me a glimpse into the past, and all I had learned was that Mom had been happier without me.

What good would it do to keep investigating? What if it just made things worse?

"I think I get what you mean about families," I said. "Like, families that overcome stuff together end up being stronger. But what if that doesn't happen? What if instead of bringing us together, our problems just tear my family apart?"

Mr. Taylor stared at the picture over the mantel for a long moment. When he turned his gaze back to me, his eyes shone. He placed one of his hands—freckled and gnarled and scarred in several places—on mine.

"Family is the most important thing we have, Miranda. It's the best gift we're given. It's true that some people have to make their own families in life, but I don't think you're one of them."

We could hear Sammy's and Caleb's footsteps creaking back toward the living room.

"And Miranda?" said Mr. Taylor. "Don't be afraid to tell your friends what you're going through. They're another kind of family, you know. Trust them. Let them help you. That's what families are for."

That night, I told Aunt Clare about my idea for a raspberry-lemonade pie.

"That sounds perfect, Miranda!" she said, clapping her hands together. "Very original. And I've already got raspberries in the fridge from our berry pie, and lemons left over from the lemon chiffon. What do you think? Want to give it a try?"

We came up with the recipe as we went, making a lemon curd out of lemon juice, eggs, sugar, and butter, then stirring in chopped raspberries. While the pie baked, we made a raspberry meringue to go on top.

It was the best pie yet, with crust as light as a cloud and filling that tasted like the end of summer—a tart sweetness that stayed on our tongues long after we were done.

"Brava!" Uncle Amar cried as he swallowed his first bite. "This is *truly* the best pie I've ever tasted."

"You totally have to bake this one for the contest," Sammy said. "There's no way it won't win."

"I want another slice," said Jai.

"Me too," echoed Caleb. "It's even better than the ice cream."

They all started to clap, and I stood and held the edges of my apron out in a little curtsy. When I looked up, I caught Caleb looking at me, and felt a blush shoot into my cheeks that made them tingle.

After dinner, when Sammy and Caleb were downstairs fighting over what movie to watch and Jai was in his room, talking on the phone as usual, I slipped upstairs to the roof. I hadn't let myself think about what Mr. Taylor said while I was making my pie. But his words had been rattling around my head while we ate dinner.

He seemed so sure that whatever was broken between Mom and me wasn't my fault. If there was any chance he was right, that I was missing something—something that had nothing to do with me—I needed to know.

I pulled out my phone and stared down at the blank screen. My palms were sweating. I started to type a text to Mom, then stopped. I wasn't exactly sure what I was going to say to her, but whatever it was, I didn't think it was the kind of thing you could really say over text.

Instead I dialed her number. It rang and rang. And then, just as I had decided it had been stupid to think that she might actually pick up, she did.

"Hi, sweetie!" Mom said, her voice cheerful. "You must have ESP. I was just thinking about you. How's it going there?"

The line was much better than it had been the last time we'd talked, so I could hear her voice loud and clear. For a second, I even thought I caught her scent on the breeze, which made my heart pinch with longing.

"Hi, Mom," I said, curling my knees up under my chin. "I'm good."

"Having fun?"

"A lot," I said, hesitating. I still wanted to keep the sailing lessons a surprise, but I also wanted to show Mom that I wasn't the same Miranda I had been a few weeks ago.

"I've been riding the roller coaster at the amusement park," I said. "And Aunt Clare has been helping me learn to make pies. I'm actually kind of good at it now."

There was a pause. Long enough for me to realize that the only thing I wanted more than Mom to know I was changing was for her to tell me I didn't need to.

"Well, that's great, honey," she said finally. "I know how much you've been wanting to learn to bake."

The longing was suddenly replaced by strange heat that quivered in my chest like a second heart.

That's great? I know how much you've been wanting to learn to bake?

If she really knew that, why hadn't she ever helped me? So maybe she *wasn't* the kind of mom who baked. But couldn't she just do that one thing for me?

"I saw your name today," I said sharply. "It was written in the sidewalk with Aunt Clare's. And with the name Ben."

Another pause. The wind blew, and this time it smelled only like salt.

"Did you?" Mom said finally.

"Who's Ben?"

"Oh, I . . . don't really remember." Her voice was flat and uncertain. Like quicksand.

"I guess you had lots of friends when you were here," I said. "Maybe he was one of them."

"Probably," Mom said. "So how are you liking—"

"Why did you stop coming to August Isle?"

"What?"

"If you were so happy here, why did you stop coming? Why wouldn't you ever take me to visit?"

I heard her take a deep breath. "Life gets busy. You'll understand when you get older."

{ 185 }

"Sammy wants us both to come visit," I said. "Will you come?"

"Miranda, you're acting very strange," Mom said. "Why don't we talk about this when you get home? I want to know more about what you've been doing there."

My knuckles wrapped tighter around my phone. Why wouldn't she answer a single one of my questions?

"Maybe I'll just ask Aunt Clare who Ben is," I said.

"Don't do that, Miranda. If I don't remember, I'm sure she doesn't either."

"Then why does it matter?"

"Because I asked you not to." Mom's voice was suddenly icy. "I don't know what's gotten into you tonight. It seems like you're trying to upset me."

"To ruin things like I always do, you mean?"

"What?"

"Do you even miss me, Mom? Do you even want to come home?"

"Miranda, what are you—"

Any second, I knew, I would burst into tears. And I couldn't let Mom hear me cry. "Just never mind," I said, my words beginning to wobble. "You probably need to get back to your work anyway. Sorry I'm such a burden."

She started to say something, but I hung up before I could hear what it was.

29

At *first, the tears* that came were burning hot and angry, like fire ants scurrying down my cheeks.

But then my anger ran out, and they became tears of sorrow. Regret tugged at my heart. What had I done? I hadn't meant to get so angry. I didn't even know I *was* angry.

Now everything had crumbled in my hands like a piecrust gripped too tight.

I stared at my phone, willing the screen to light up with the word "Mom." But it stayed dark.

What if I had finally pushed her too far, and she really did stay gone this time?

Please don't forget me.

Please come home.

Why had I listened to Mr. Taylor in the first place? Why did I think Ben or August Isle or any of it would have anything to do with why things were broken between Mom and me?

"Miranda?" came Sammy's voice. "Miranda, what's wrong?"

When I looked up, I saw her standing across the rooftop, by the stairs. Caleb hovered behind her. "You okay?" he asked.

I started to nod but then stopped and shook my head instead. Fresh tears rose as they sat down in the chairs on either side of me.

"What is it?" Sammy tried again, alarmed.

"It's my m-mom," I stammered.

"Is something wrong with her?" Caleb asked. "Is she okay?"

"She's fine," I said, sniffling and wiping my cheeks with my wrists. "It's me. I'm the one there's something wrong with."

"What are you talking about?" Sammy asked.

My heart began to race. I had never told anyone the truth about Mom before.

They were both staring at me, though, eyes round with concern. And I decided that even if Mr. Taylor's advice about Mom hadn't worked out very well, he *was* right about one thing. I could trust Sammy and

Caleb. I *needed* to trust them.

"My mom and I don't, um, have a great relationship," I mumbled.

Then everything was spilling out. I told them how I remembered a time when Mom's love felt big as the sun, but how its heat had faded away. I told them how much happier she looked in the pictures taken at August Isle than she ever did at home with me, and how every time she left on another trip, a little part of me wondered if she would actually come home again.

When I couldn't talk anymore, the three of us sat in silence for a minute, the ocean humming in our ears.

Then I felt Sammy's arm around my shoulders, squeezing it tight. "I'm so sorry," she whispered.

"Yeah. That's really tough," Caleb murmured. He reached out and patted my head, which was sweet, even if it did make me feel a little like Slug.

"It's my fault," I said. "I'm always ruining stuff."

Sammy made a sizzling sound. "You don't ruin anything, Miranda. Whatever's going on with your mom, it's not your fault."

"I ruined our first sailing lessons," I pointed out. "And tons of pies. And it's my fault that we got caught in Mr. Taylor's house."

"You're scared of water!" Sammy exclaimed. "Obviously you were afraid to go sailing at first. But you've been really brave ever since. And your pie tonight was, like, the best pie ever. Caleb had three slices!"

"And Mr. Taylor's house turned out to be pretty cool," Caleb said. "Sammy's right. This summer would have been a total borefest without you."

"Your parents think I'm a burden," I said to Sammy. "I heard them talking about it."

Sammy made a face and shook her head. "No way," she said. "They would never say that. You must have misheard them. Seriously, Miranda, they love you! They don't think you're a burden, and I'm sure your mom doesn't either."

I shrugged. I wanted to believe Sammy, but I'd heard them with my own ears.

"I don't know. I just think—maybe things would be better between my mom and me if I were different. More like you."

My eyes swiveled toward Sammy.

"Me?" she asked.

"You and your parents get along so great," I said. "You never fight. You never disappoint them. You make things easier for your family, not harder."

"That's not always true," Sammy said quietly.

"I'm not talking about flunking a math quiz," I said.

"Neither am I."

"So what do you mean?" Caleb asked.

Sammy ran her fingers through her hair and tugged

at the ends. "If you tell *anyone* at school what I'm going to say to you," she said, turning and jabbing Caleb in the chest, "I will never speak to you again. Got it?"

Caleb held up his hands. "Got it."

"Fine." She took a deep breath. "Well, people have gotten my name wrong sometimes, and when I brought dal or chole or other Indian food to school, usually someone would say it looked weird or smelled bad. Things like that. But in fifth grade, there was this new kid, Roger. He started spreading all these mean rumors about what was in my food and what India is like and stuff. And then other kids started teasing me more."

"I remember that," Caleb muttered.

"Yeah, well, I was really upset, and I told my mom about it, and she got really upset, too. She wanted to call the school and Roger's parents, but I told her that would just make things worse, and later that night I heard her crying with my dad, talking about how they just felt so helpless to protect me. And that's when I decided to do something. So I wouldn't get made fun of anymore."

"You mean like change your name?" I said softly. I laced my fingers through hers and squeezed.

She nodded. "I only brought sandwiches for lunch, and whenever anyone asked me anything about India,

I pretended like I didn't know. When we had to do a project on another country in social studies, I picked Italy. I just didn't want people to be able to hurt my feelings anymore. Or my mom's and dad's." She lifted her chin up in the air and did her best to sound casual, but I could see that her lower lip was trembling.

"Then last summer we went back to Mumbai, and it was, like, the best trip ever. My family and the city and the food and the clothes . . . it was all so awesome. But sometimes I got this feeling that I didn't really belong there either. There was just so much I didn't know. And some of my cousins told me they saw our dadi get mad at Dad because Jai and I couldn't speak any Punjabi, and she couldn't believe I didn't know how to make any of her recipes."

"You do now," I said. "You help your dad cook all the time!"

"Yeah, well, that trip made me realize how much I love being Indian. I love being American, too. I want to belong there, *and* I want to belong here. But it's like I'm not enough for either place. Like I just end up upsetting everybody."

"Sammy, no!" I cried. I couldn't believe that Sammy—whose confidence I had wished for, whose family I had envied—could ever feel like this. "You can't think like that. You're totally enough, and your family loves you!"

"I know that in my head," Sammy said. "But some-times it's hard to feel it in my heart."

"I'm so sorry," I said, wrapping my arms around her. "It's not fair that you have to feel like that."

"It's really not," Caleb said.

"I know that," Sammy replied, her voice quiet. "It's Roger and your other friends who don't seem to get it."

"You're *friends* with that guy?" I said.

Caleb grimaced. "Yeah," he replied. "He's kind of my friend. I mean, we don't hang out that much any-more, but . . . maybe I could talk with him? Tell him that it's not cool to make fun of you. Especially not if it's because you're Indian."

Sammy eyed him for a minute. Then she nodded. "That would be good," she said finally, sniffling. "Thanks."

"I still can't believe you could ever think that you weren't enough for your family," I said.

"I can't believe *you* think that either. How could you think your mom would be happier with a different family?"

"I know mine would be," Caleb muttered.

We turned to look at him. He was sitting cross-legged, staring down at the floor.

"What are you talking about?" Sammy asked.

"Well . . . my parents are kind of, um, getting divorced," Caleb said. "Only my dad hasn't moved out yet, so right now they're just fighting and yelling all the time."

"Oh," I breathed. In an instant, I understood why he never seemed to want to go home. Whenever I heard Mom and Dad arguing in their room, I got a nervous feeling in the pit of my stomach. I couldn't imagine what it would be like if they fought all the time. And I remembered how Caleb had snapped at me after we heard the story about Inkeri, who ran away so she wouldn't have to marry someone she didn't love. It all made sense now.

"Sometimes I've wondered whether, if they had a different kid, like a better kid, or maybe even no kid at all, they might still be happy together. And this last year, I tried to be so good in school and stuff, hoping that it would help. That's why I stopped hanging out with Roger and those guys. But it didn't make a difference. How could it? My parents were too busy fighting to even notice me." Caleb glanced up at us and smiled, but it looked like a smile cut out of cardboard.

"I'm really sorry, Caleb."

"Me too," Sammy said.

"It's okay. After a while, you realize that anything is better than the fighting. I'm just scared that my dad will move away. Or get a new family, you know? That always happens in movies."

I reached over and patted him the way he had done

to me. He didn't seem to think it was weird at all.

"I wish we had told each other this stuff earlier," I said after a minute. "I bet we all would have felt less lonely."

"It's funny, isn't it?" Caleb said. "All three of us have felt bad about stuff we have no control over. Stuff our parents chose."

"You sound exactly like Mr. Taylor today," I said. I told them about the adinkra cloth, and the sankofa in the gate, and how it meant not being afraid to look into your past.

"So I asked my mom about that name we saw in the sidewalk," I said. "Ben. And she told me she didn't remember him. But she sounded really strange."

"You mean you think she was lying?" Sammy asked.

I bit my lip. "The thing is, whenever I ask a question about this place, she always says she doesn't remember. I didn't even know it existed until Sammy came to visit."

Caleb nodded knowingly. "Sounds like she's definitely keeping a secret."

"Let's just ask my mom about Ben," Sammy said.

I shook my head. "My mom told me I shouldn't. If we ask, your mom will probably just tell my mom, and then she'll be even more upset."

"Then we have to find another way," Sammy said. "Because I think Mr. Taylor is right, Miranda."

"What do you mean?"

"Well, you act like you're this horrible daughter, but nobody else seems to think you're so terrible. I think you're kind of great."

"Me too," mumbled Caleb.

I felt a little flurry in my stomach.

"So maybe there *is* another reason your mom acts so weird. And maybe it has to do with this Ben person. But it *definitely* has to do with August Isle."

"But what would something that happened here have to do with the way things are between her and me?" I asked. "I've never set foot in this place before this summer."

"I don't know," Sammy mused. "We won't ever know unless we figure out what the secret is. Which is why we need to find out more about this Ben guy."

I crossed my arms over my chest. If Mom found out I was investigating the mysterious Ben, she'd be furious. Or worse, disappointed.

But if Sammy was right, then I had to know. That's why I had called Mom in the first place, wasn't it?

"Let me think about it," I said. "I'm not—"

But I stopped short. The hairs at the back of my neck prickled.

"What's wrong?" Sammy asked.

"Shh," I said. "Look."

I stared at the ink blot in the ocean that was Keeper's

Island. For a second, there was just the wind and the waves. Then I saw a soft light burning from the top of the lighthouse. After a moment, the sound came again. The cry. High and long, almost like a scream.

Sammy gave a little gasp, and Caleb's jaw fell open.

"See?" I whispered. "Told you I wasn't imagining things."

30

After Caleb went home that night, Sammy and I stayed up late, whispering about Keeper's Island. "Why is someone sneaking around out there at night?" Sammy asked. "No one *ever* goes there."

"I don't know," I replied. "But I have a feeling you finally found your scoop."

"I can already see the headline," she said. "'Keeper's Island: The Shocking Truth Behind the Legend.'"

And we weren't the only ones thinking about Sammy's story.

When we came down for breakfast the next morning, Aunt Clare was flipping pancakes. She looked over her shoulder at us, and for just a second, a frown flitted across her face. Then she was smiling and telling us good morning.

"How's your article coming, Sammy?" she asked, setting our plates down at the table.

Aunt Clare still thought we were spending our afternoons at the library and interviewing people for Sammy's article. Which, as far as she knew, was still about sea turtles.

Sammy shot me a glance. "Good," she said. "Actually, really good. I think I'm on to something."

Now Aunt Clare sat down across the table from us. "You've been spending an awful lot of time on this story. I can't wait to read it."

"It's going to be great," I said, nervously stuffing a bite of chocolate-chip pancake into my mouth.

"I'm sure," Aunt Clare replied. "But I don't want you running around the Isle on your own anymore. Not without supervision."

"Why?" Sammy and I asked.

"Apparently a few people have been pickpocketed on Oak Street this week," she replied. She wasn't looking either of us in the eye. "I don't think it's safe for the three of you to walk around alone."

"I haven't heard anything about any pickpockets," Sammy retorted.

"Well, you don't watch the evening news. Now, let's go. We're late for your lesson."

Sammy shot me a dark look, but not until Aunt Clare let us out at the sailing beach could we talk about what had happened.

"I think my mom called yours, Sammy," I said, once Caleb had arrived and we'd filled him in. "Last night. She must have told Aunt Clare about Ben. Told her to keep an eye on us so we couldn't investigate."

"I was thinking the same thing," Sammy said as we tugged on our life jackets. "Well, at least we know for sure that you were right, Miranda. Your mom is definitely keeping a secret from you, and my mom is helping her. But how are we going to figure out what it is if my mom won't let us go out on our own?"

"If Miranda even wants to find out," Caleb said. His voice sounded froggy and tired. "Do you?"

"I don't know," I said. Which wasn't quite true. Of course I *wanted* to know what Mom was hiding. I just didn't know if it was worth the risk of Mom finding out I had gone behind her back.

Oh, Miranda, she said in my head. *How could you?*

My heart had sunk that morning when I'd seen the blank screen on my phone. I had half expected her to call or text or something. She must be really angry at me already.

And then there was another voice in my head. The one that said that maybe Mom had a reason for keeping secrets from me. And maybe it was a good one.

"How would we even find Ben?" I asked. "There must be a million Bens in the world."

"Maybe we could start by asking the people who live in the houses near where the names are written," Sammy said. "Maybe someone there will know who he is."

Once we got out onto the water—Sammy and I sharing a boat today—her attention turned back to her own investigation. She kept peering out at Keeper's Island. I could almost see her mind churning with ideas.

Suddenly she turned the tiller, and we cut through the water toward Caleb and Jason's boat.

"Jason?" she called. "Can we sail out there one day?"

Jason looked where Sammy was pointing. "You mean to Keeper's Island?" he asked. "No can do, Captain. We're not allowed. But I thought after the August Festival, we could finally sail out of the harbor. Maybe even have a little regatta. What do you say, Miranda?"

"Is it because of the legend?" Sammy asked before I could reply. "About the ghost? Is that why we can't go?"

Jason laughed, his teeth bright white against his tanned skin. "Well, that," he said, "and it's private property. If you ever get close enough, you'll see the Keep Out signs in the water all around it."

"Who owns it?" Caleb asked.

Jason tugged the brim of his baseball cap lower over his face. "Not sure, dude. Someone with a lot more money than me, I guess."

"Nobody lives there, right?" Sammy asked.

He shook his head.

"But does anyone ever visit?" I tried.

"I've never seen anyone out there. Why so many questions?"

"I'm writing an article about the island," Sammy said.

"Hmmm," Jason murmured. "Well, I hate to break it to you, but there's no getting onto Keeper's Island." Then he grinned. "And besides, the old keeper is waiting for his next victim. You don't want it to be you."

Maybe it was just because the sun was so bright, but I swore I saw Sammy's eyes narrow the tiniest bit, like Jason had thrown down a challenge.

And she had accepted.

"Why didn't you tell him about what we saw last night?" I whispered, once we had sailed away again.

"When you have a scoop, you don't just go around blabbing about it to everyone," she said.

A trio of pelicans flew overhead. We watched as they dove, beaks first, into the water nearby. A few seconds later, they emerged. One of them had a shiny fish flopping in its beak.

"So what now?" I asked.

Sammy thought for a minute. "Find out who owns it, maybe?"

"Or you could talk to Mr. Taylor."

"Mr. Taylor?"

"Yeah. I mean, wasn't he supposed to be the ghost's last victim? Obviously, he wasn't, but maybe there's a reason the rumor got started. Maybe he knows something about the island. He might have been there, at least."

Sammy clapped her palms to her cheeks. "Miranda, that's genius! Why didn't I think of that? *You* would make a good reporter, too."

"I don't know about that," I said. But I was glad that I had been able to help Sammy, even just a little. "How are we going to get to his house today? Without your mom knowing?"

Sammy's face broke into a smile, the sun catching blindingly on her braces. "I think I have an idea."

31

For Sammy's plan to work, we needed Jai's help.

The three of us cornered him after lunch, when he was about to leave for his lifeguarding shift and Aunt Clare was upstairs getting ready for her lessons. Sammy laid it all out for him in one long breath.

We would tell Aunt Clare we were going to the beach, where Jai could look after us. We would even leave towels and a beach bag just in case she came to check on us after her lessons were done. If that happened, Jai would tell her we had gone for a walk. He would text us, and we would leave Mr. Taylor's and cut back over to the beach.

"No way," Jai scoffed.

"Please, Jai?" Sammy begged. "Please, please, please?"

He started for the front door. "Why would I lie to Mom for you?"

"I'll trade you. I'll do your chores for two weeks."

Jai stopped, his hand on the doorknob. Sammy bit her lip and looked upstairs, listening for any sign of Aunt Clare.

"And clean the bathroom?" he asked.

Sammy gave a disgusted sigh. "Fine."

"For a month," he said.

She crossed her arms over her chest. "Only if you cover for us tomorrow, too."

Jai hesitated. Then he shrugged. "Whatever," he said. "But you have to tell me what you guys are doing."

Sammy and I glanced at each other. For once, it seemed she didn't have a story ready to roll off her tongue. It was Caleb who spoke.

"They're helping me. My parents are, um, getting divorced. My dad moved to a hotel last night, and I have to bring some stuff to him. The thing is, they don't want anyone to know they're splitting up yet, so we can't really tell your mom."

The sharp angles of Jai's face softened. "Oh," he said. "Sorry, man."

He hesitated another second before shrugging. "Fine," he said. "But if you get caught, I'm telling Mom I had no idea."

Sammy ignored him, clapping her hands together as the door slammed shut behind Jai. "That was awesome, Caleb!" she said. "How did you come up with that so fast?"

"I didn't," he said, and I realized that he had big purple circles under his eyes. "My dad *did* move to a hotel last night."

"Oh, no," Sammy breathed.

"I'm really sorry, Caleb," I said. "Are you okay?"

"Yeah," he replied. "Honestly. At least they can't fight while my dad stays there. And at least he's close by. For now."

I didn't say anything, but having your dad live in a hotel didn't sound very okay to me. It sounded awful.

"Come on, Miranda," said Sammy after a minute. "Let's go tell my mom we're going to the beach."

But my feet stayed planted where they were.

"What's wrong?" Sammy asked.

It was bad enough, I thought, that I couldn't have a normal relationship with my own mom. But now I was jeopardizing Sammy's relationship with hers. Didn't Caleb's dad moving out just go to show how fragile families could be? That not all families could work through their problems?

"Are you sure you want to lie to your mom?" I asked. "I don't want to make trouble for you guys after everything you've done for me. I mean, won't you feel bad about it?"

But Sammy just blinked. "Why would I?" she replied. "She's been lying to me, hasn't she? I checked online, and there's nothing about people being pickpocketed in town."

When Sammy started upstairs, I followed her. Because when she put it that way, it didn't seem quite so wrong.

It was Mr. Taylor who came to the door that after-noon.

"Where's Betsy?" Sammy asked, as we stepped in.

"Ladrão!" Safira cawed.

"She had to take care of her mother today," Mr. Taylor said. "I guess she wasn't feeling well this morning, so Betsy took her to the doctor. She gets confused quite easily these days, I gather."

"That's too bad," Sammy said. Then she spotted Slug, his tail thumping against the living-room rug. There was something different about him today. "Hey! His cone is gone!"

"Yes, he's all healed up," Mr. Taylor said. "As they

say, time heals all wounds. Shall we get started? I think we'll finish it today."

His last words hung over us like storm clouds as we all stared at the last two lonely boxes.

"Does this mean it's our last day here?" I asked.

"Actually, I was thinking maybe we could have a kind of—party," he said. "Before Miranda leaves. To say thank you for all your help. But if you have other plans, of course—"

"Can we do it tomorrow?" Sammy asked.

"Not tomorrow," Mr. Taylor said. "I've got some errands to run on the mainland. And the next day is the August Festival, so I expect you'll be busy."

"Will you be there?" I asked.

He shook his head. "I'm not much of a crowd person. But perhaps the next day? You can come over around lunchtime, and I'll have Betsy make us something special."

"That's the day before I leave," I said, my stomach twisting.

I thought I saw a flicker of sorrow dart through Mr. Taylor's gray eyes, quick as a swallow flitting past on the wind.

"Don't remind me," Sammy groaned, glancing up from a sleeping Slug, whose tongue lolled in a long ribbon to the floor.

"We'll be here," I said.

She glanced at me. We would have to convince Jai to cover for us another day. Maybe Sammy could offer to do his laundry or something.

I looked around the room. Dust no longer danced in the air, and the damp smell from before had been mostly replaced with something like cinnamon. It looked so bare without all the crates.

"Can I ask a question?" I said.

"Of course."

"What did you do with all the stuff you brought back? And what's going to happen to all the stories? Why'd you have me type them all?"

Mr. Taylor settled down in his usual place on the couch, and Safira hopped over to him. "I thought I would put them somewhere," he said. "Someplace where people can see the objects and learn their stories."

"You mean, like, a museum?" Caleb asked.

"Of sorts."

"What about *your* story?" Sammy asked. "Is it going in the museum?"

"So many questions today," he said, arching his eyebrows.

"Will you at least tell *us* your story today?" Sammy tried.

Mr. Taylor shot her a tired smile. "You'll make a great journalist," he said. "You're quite—persistent.

But I'm afraid the answer is not today. Now, shall we—"

"Actually, can I ask one more question?" Sammy interrupted.

Mr. Taylor's smile fell into a hesitant frown. "Yes?"

"It's about how, um, how you left August Isle."

"So you want to know about ancient history, then?" His voice was light, but I thought I saw his jaw stiffen beneath his beard.

"The night Miranda, um, broke in here," Sammy said, "it was because Caleb dared her to. Because we didn't think you would be here."

"Because we thought you were dead," added Caleb.

"And why would you think that?"

"Because of the legend. You know, the one about the ghost of the lighthouse keeper?"

Mr. Taylor crossed his arms over his chest. Three little lines appeared in his forehead. "I know the legend."

"Well, people said that's why you disappeared," Sammy explained. "They said that you went to Keeper's Island and the ghost got you."

"Did they, now?"

"Yes. And I want to write an article about Keeper's Island. And I wondered—because of the legend—if maybe you knew anything about it?"

"Unfortunately," said Mr. Taylor, "I don't think I'll

be of much help to you, since—as you can see—I was not, in fact, murdered by a vengeful ghost. I'm sorry to be so uninteresting."

Sammy sighed. Then, "It's okay," she said. "There *is* a story there. And I'm going to find it, just like you found all these." She tapped the lid of one of the remaining boxes.

For a few seconds, Mr. Taylor just stared at her. "I believe you will, Sammy," he said finally. "But first, I think we have one or two last stories waiting for us here."

33

The very last place the wind blew me on my travels was to Lima, Peru, a city overlooking the Pacific from its perch upon ragged clifftops. One evening, after a long day walking through its winding streets, I stopped in a park to watch the sun set over the sea.

Presently a woman sat down on my bench. With her was a small, pigtailed girl who waved shyly at me before running off to play.

Her mother and I soon struck up a conversation. She asked me where I was from and why I was visiting Lima. When she caught sight of her daughter trying to scale a nearby tree, she scolded her. "No, Illari!"

"Is that her name?" I asked.

"Yes," she said "She is named for my grand-mother."

"Your grandmother must have been a special person," I said.

"She was," the woman replied. "Very special."

"I'd love to hear about her, if you have the time," I said.

The woman studied me curiously for a moment.

"My grandmother came to live with my father and me when my mother died," she began. "I was only ten years old then, and I did not know how to live without a mother.

"At first, when my grandmother came, I found her very strange. I had grown up in the city. She had grown up in an ancient village high in the Andes. I thought she was backward, and she thought I was much too modern. One night, she woke to hear me crying. When she asked me what was wrong, I told her I missed my mother. That I could no longer feel her love.

"My grandmother told me then what her grand-mother had told her as a child. That people are simply stars, fallen from the sky. We live our lives here on earth, and when we are ready, we return to our place in the heavens. 'So do not cry, my child,' she whispered. 'For your mother's love shines down on you always.'

"At first, I did not believe my grandmother. I thought she was just telling me a story. But soon I began to find my mother everywhere. Her favorite song played in the shops I went into. In every book I read, I found her name. The flowers she had planted years before bloomed again in the spring. And slowly, my anger faded. For I found that my grandmother was right. Though I could not see my mother any longer, she was with me all the time, like a star that becomes invisible when the sun rises but is always there, hanging in the sky.

"My grandmother lived a long time, and we grew to be very good friends. The night after she died, I took a bus away from the city lights and lay in a field, looking up at the stars. Just as my eyes began to close, I glimpsed one of them falling to earth. And I remembered what my grandmother had said. The very next day, I found out I was going to have a baby. I knew then that it would be a girl, and we would name her Illari, after my grandmother."

"Do you truly believe what she told you?" I asked after a moment. "About the stars, I mean?"

"My grandmother's ancestors believed we fell from the stars for thousands of years before science

proved that our bodies are made of stardust,"
the woman said. "Is it so hard to believe that
they might have understood something else
about what happens when we die? Who am I
not to believe? And who, for that matter, are
you?"

"That's the very last story?" Sammy asked, once Mr. Taylor was finished.

"The last one I collected before coming home," he said, staring down at the photograph Sammy had pulled from the final box. It showed the silhouette of a woman with a little girl hoisted on her hip, both of them watching the sun go down over the ocean.

"Isn't there something else that goes with it?" Caleb asked. "A painting or a sculpture or something?"

"Just the photo," said Mr. Taylor. "Real love is something you feel, but it's not something you can touch or hold. Which means nothing can take it from you, see? Not even death. That's what the woman in the story learned."

"Do you think her grandmother sent that falling star?" Sammy asked. "That she sent the baby?"

Mr. Taylor didn't answer for a minute. "I suppose I believe that when a person loves you, their love continues to echo on, even after they're gone." He cleared his throat and stood up. "I'm feeling a bit tired now. I think I'll go lie down. Caleb, why don't you take the giveaway book pile over to the library now? I'll see you all soon."

As we got up to leave, though, I didn't think Mr. Taylor looked very tired.

I just thought he looked sad.

34

Caleb went to lug Mr. Taylor's huge box of books to the library. Sammy and I thought we should start heading back to get our stuff on the beach, so we went in the opposite direction.

Sammy was the first to find her voice. "Do you know anyone who died?" she asked.

"Only my grandparents on my mom's side," I said as we climbed the boardwalk stairs. Sandy dunes covered in sea grass rose up like tiny mountains on either side of us. In the distance, I could see the orange ribbons around the sea turtle's nest. "But they died before I was born, so I never met them. What about you?"

"My granddad on my dad's side died when I was ten," she said. "I didn't get to go to his funeral, though, because it was in India. Only my dad went."

I usually tried not to think about death. Whenever I did, I thought about Mom or Dad dying and never being able to talk to them or see them again. Then I would get this awful panicky feeling in my chest, and if I wasn't with them, I would have to text them just to make sure they were okay.

"Do you think your granddad is up there somewhere?" I pointed to the sky, where fat seagulls flew over our heads, camouflaged by the clouds.

"Well, Hindus believe in reincarnation," Sammy said. "It's called samsara. You live all these different lives, but your soul—your atman—stays the same. So my grandfather wouldn't be up in the stars. He would be here on earth, living a totally new life."

"Whoa," I said. "So would he know who you were if he saw you?"

Sammy shook her head. "It doesn't really work like that. You don't get to carry your memories. Just your karma. All your good deeds and bad deeds. They come back to you in the next life."

"More echoes," I said. "Like Mr. Taylor was talking about."

We reached the spot where we had laid our beach towels down, near Jai's lifeguard tower. A blond girl with a big sun hat was chatting up at him, and he was laughing at something she said. I wondered if she was the one he was always talking to on the phone at night.

Just then, I felt my own phone vibrating in my pocket. My heart pounded as I reached back to get it.

It wasn't Mom, though. It was Dad. Maybe it was because of what we'd just been talking about, but I was really happy he was calling.

"Hello?" I said, walking a few paces toward the surf.

"There she is!" said Dad. "How are you, kiddo?"

"I'm okay, I guess," I said, letting my toes sink into the sand. A line of creamy seashells rattled against the waves a few inches away. "How are you?"

"Oh, I'm okay, too."

My throat tightened. I could tell by the sigh in his voice that he had talked to Mom. But what had she told him?

It suddenly occurred to me to wonder if Mom was keeping secrets from Dad, too, or just me. I hadn't thought about it before. I waited for him to speak.

"Your mom said you had a talk that didn't go very well last night," he said.

"Is she mad?"

"She's upset. I know you are, too. We're all going to have to sit down and have a talk when you're both home. I think there's a lot we need to discuss. Actually, I was wondering if—"

A pause.

"If what?"

"If maybe you should come home early," Dad said. "It's not ideal—you'd have to come stay in the hotel here until Mom gets back, but we could make it work for a few days."

"NO!" I cried, toes cringing in the sand. "No, Dad, please. I want to stay. It's the August Festival the day after tomorrow and I'm supposed to enter the pie contest, and Sammy needs my help with her article and—and—"

"Okay, kiddo," Dad said. "Okay. You can stay. It was just a suggestion. But if you really want to . . ."

"I do," I said. "I really do."

"Then like I said, we'll talk when you get home. But until then?" There was another pause. "Just—leave things be. Just concentrate on having fun. All right? Can you do that for me?"

I felt cold then, even though the air was oven hot. So Mom wasn't keeping secrets from Dad. Mom and Dad were *both* keeping secrets from me.

"Kiddo?"

"Okay," I said numbly.

"Good. And Miranda? I want you to know that— that I love you. And so does your mom. Very much."

There was something strange about the way he said it. Like maybe he was speaking in a language he didn't know very well and he wasn't sure he'd used the right words.

After he hung up, I stared out at the ocean for a moment—the threads of blue and white and green weaving together and blowing apart again. When I looked down, the line of seashells had disappeared, drawn out by the tide.

I suddenly wished that I had thought to lean down and scoop one up before they had been pulled away. By now, they would probably be deep on the ocean floor where no one would see them again for a long time. Years, maybe. Or perhaps they would stay hidden forever.

Next to me, a sandpiper scurried around on its straw-thin legs. First it ran toward the water. Then, when the next wave came rushing in, it whirled away again. Back and forth it scuttled, making its mind up and then changing it again just as quickly.

It reminded me of Mom. Always coming home, just to fly off again. Always running away.

I realized something then. Something that surprised me so much, it sent a jolt through me, like when you walk around a corner and you don't realize someone is coming from the other direction until you nearly run into them.

I loved Mom, and I wanted her to love me as fiercely as I loved her.

But I didn't want to be *like* her.

I didn't want to be the sandpiper, zigzagging back and forth, always on the move, unable to make up its mind.

I liked hearing Mr. Taylor's stories about all the places he had traveled and the people he had met. But if his stories were the closest I ever got to traveling the world, I would be okay with that.

I wanted to be like the August Oak, silently stretching its roots deeper and farther into the ground and gripping the earth, listening and watching, feeling my branches blowing in the wind but never floating away on it.

And maybe that wasn't such a bad thing to want. Trees were strong and steady, even in the face of storms. Without trees to come home to, there probably wouldn't *be* any birds.

Then I realized something else.

I had started out the summer thinking that, if I could change myself enough, Mom might love me how she used to.

But somewhere along the way, I had started changing for *me*, too. Because I liked feeling proud after every sailing lesson. I liked watching people eat the pies I had made. I liked the way it felt not to be afraid and worried all the time.

And I didn't want to be afraid of Mom's secret anymore. I couldn't just let it float away on the tide. Not while I had the chance to find out what it was. Not if it might explain why Mom always chose to run instead of stay.

Whatever the secret was, I wasn't going to be like Mom. I wasn't going to run from it.

I was Miranda, brave and bold, and I was going to stay right here and face it head-on.

35

Caleb met us back at Sammy's house later that afternoon. When she opened the door, he was holding an old picture book.

Sammy looked at it and giggled. "I don't think that's what Mrs. Kleinfield had in mind when she said we needed to do independent reading over the summer."

Caleb rolled his eyes and handed it to her. "The library wouldn't take this one," he said in a low voice, so Aunt Clare wouldn't overhear. "I guess it's too worn out. We can give it back to him when we go for the party thing."

Once we were excused from dinner that night, Sammy led us into the garage, where we rummaged around until she found a pair of binoculars in Jai's old Boy Scout stuff. Then we went up to the roof.

She held the binoculars to her eyes, gazing out toward Keeper's Island as darkness began to fall.

"You guys," I said, "I think I want to know who Ben is."

Sammy and Caleb turned to look at me.

"Are you sure?" he asked.

"Yeah. I am."

"I think you're making the right decision, Miranda," Sammy said, the wind whipping her hair back from her neck. "Tomorrow afternoon, we'll go back to where you saw the names, and we'll knock on the doors of the houses around there. We keep going until we find someone who knows him."

"Hey!" Caleb called. "What's that light?"

Sammy jammed the binoculars to her face.

"I don't see anything," she said. "Oh, wait. Yes I do. But it's not coming from the island. It's a ship passing behind it."

"Oh," said Caleb. "Oh, well."

"I still don't get why someone would be going out to a haunted island at night," Sammy mused, passing the binoculars to Caleb to let him have a turn.

I thought back to the night on the Ferris wheel, when Sammy and Caleb first told me the story of the lighthouse keeper, and how they swore that it was true.

"Hey," I said, "you guys told me you believed the legend. What if you aren't the only ones?"

"We're not," Caleb replied. "Lots of people do. But like Sammy said . . . if you believed it, why would you go there?"

"Think about it. Why did the lighthouse keeper get killed in the first place?"

Caleb was the first to understand. "The treasure!" he exclaimed. "He got killed by pirates coming to bury their treasure."

"So if someone believed the legend was real," Sammy reasoned, "they might think there was treasure on the island."

"And they might sail out there at night," I said, "when they thought no one was watching, to try and find it for themselves."

"It's possible," Sammy said. "So what makes that awful sound?"

"Maybe some kind of machinery?" I suggested. "Like for digging?"

"Do you guys think there *is* treasure out there?" Caleb asked. The brightening moon glittered in his eyes.

Sammy shrugged. "Maybe. At least there could have been at one time. But someone could definitely *think* there was treasure out there. And then"—Sammy's face broke into a grin—"this could be a major story.

Forget about the school newspaper! I could publish it in the *Isle Tides*."

"Yeah, but how do we find out if we're right?" I asked.

"We start with the library," she said. "We'll go tomorrow and see if we can find some proof that there's any truth to the legend. And we need to find out who owns that island."

"I can do that," Caleb said.

"Really?" Sammy and I asked in unison.

"Easy. My dad knows all about that stuff for his job. He can help me."

Just then, we heard a glass door opening and Aunt Clare calling from the porch below. "Girls? I think it's time for Caleb to go home now."

"Okay," Sammy called. Caleb gave us a salute.

"See you tomorrow," I said.

Sammy and I stayed on the roof for a while longer, keeping our eyes trained on the island. But it was dark and quiet as a grave. Finally, when my eyes were tired from looking and we started passing yawns back and forth, we decided to give up for the night.

A few minutes later, when we were tucked into our beds and Sammy had turned the lights out, I heard her roll over to face me. "Miranda?" she whispered.

"Yeah?"

"We're going to get some answers tomorrow," she said. "I can feel it."

After sailing the next day, Aunt Clare dropped the
three of us off at the library. Sammy had told her that
we needed to do more research there for Sammy's
story, which was true. We split up, each of us comb-
ing the shelves for books about local history or pirates
or ghosts.

But after an hour, none of the answers Sammy had
been so sure we would find had actually turned up.
None of the local history books mentioned pirates or
ghosts, and none of the pirate or ghost books mentioned August Isle or Keeper's Island. At lunchtime,
we gave up.

"I'm seeing my dad this afternoon," Caleb said. "At

least then we'll find out who owns the place."

After Caleb left, Sammy and I repeated our plan from the day before, telling Aunt Clare we were going to the beach and laying towels down next to Jai's lifeguard tower just in case she came to look for us. Then we started off toward the names in the sidewalk.

Halfway up the beach, there was a little group of people standing around the roped-off sea turtle's nest. They wore khaki shirts and shorts, and one of them was pulling some kind of instrument out of the sand.

"What's happening there?" I asked.

"I don't know," Sammy said. "Let's find out."

And then she was off, leaving me to wonder how it was so easy for her to talk to random adults when I already had butterflies at the thought of knocking on a stranger's door.

"Scuse me," she said, tapping the shoulder of an older woman with a single long braid hanging down over her khaki shirt. "What's going on with the nest?"

"They're hatching," the woman said, smiling kindly.

"Really?" I asked, encouraged by her friendly face. I peered down at the nest, but it just looked like sand to me. "Where are they?"

"Well, once they hatch, it takes them a while to climb up to the surface. Usually a few days. That's good, because the moon should be nice and big for them then. We think that's how baby turtles find the ocean, you know. They see the light reflecting on the water and follow it."

"Can we come see?" Sammy asked. "When they climb up?"

"Actually," the woman said, "we need volunteers to come and form a kind of human wall. So the hatchlings don't get off course." She handed Sammy a card. "Text that number, and when they're almost ready, I'll send out a message and you'll know to come."

Sammy glanced at the card. "Charlie?"

"Yeah," the woman said. "Kind of unusual, huh? My real name's Charlotte."

"Why'd you shorten it?" Sammy asked.

"Well, when I was starting out, there were hardly any female biologists. I thought it would be easier to get a job if people saw my résumé and assumed by the name that I was a man. So, Charlie."

Sammy considered this for a moment. "Do you ever wish you could go back to being Charlotte?" she asked.

Charlie looked at her in surprise. "Well, that's an interesting question," she said. "I don't think anyone's ever asked me that. I'm pretty used to Charlie by now. But I guess, if I were doing it over today, I would stick with Charlotte. I was never ashamed of being a woman. I just knew it would be really hard to get a job as one. But times are different now, and most sensible people know women make just as good scientists as men. Sometimes better."

She winked at us.

"Well, thanks, Charlie," said Sammy. "For the card. I'll text you."

"Sounds good, ah—"

She hesitated for a second before answering. Then, "Sammy," she said. "And this is Miranda."

"Nice to meet you, girls," she replied. "See you soon, I hope."

I wanted to ask Sammy how she felt about what Charlie had said about her name, but she already looked lost in thought. Anyway, my mouth had suddenly gone dry, and with every step we took, my heart seemed to beat harder. Before I knew it, we were standing there on the sidewalk, looking down at the letters carved into the concrete.

Clare

Beth

Ben

"Ready?" Sammy asked. "Let's start with that house."

She pointed to the one directly in front of us, a white house with a blue door and rosebushes out front. We linked arms, and walked up the path.

I took a deep breath and rang the doorbell.

We waited for what felt like an hour before Sammy

glanced over at the driveway. "No cars," she said. "They must not be home."

"Oh. Right."

"Let's go next door."

Next door, a girl wearing a bikini top and jean shorts answered. She looked familiar. "Yeah?"

Sammy nudged me. "Um," I mumbled, "Do you know Ben?"

She cocked an eyebrow, looking back and forth from me to Sammy. "Hey," she said, "aren't you Jai's little sister?"

I had been so nervous when she opened the door that I hadn't seen it at first, but now I recognized her as the girl in the floppy sun hat we'd seen talking to Jai the day before.

"Yeah," Sammy said. "Do you live here?"

"No," said the girl, crossing her arms. "I'm just babysitting. What was it you wanted?"

"Never mind," Sammy said, before I could embarrass myself more.

"Whatever," the girl muttered, flicking the door shut.

Sammy turned to look at me. *Do you know Ben?* she asked.

"What was I supposed to say?"

"A few more details might be helpful at the next house."

"Okay," I said. "Details."

But no one was home at the next two houses. As we headed to the other side of the street, I was starting to think that our plan hadn't been much of a plan at all. What were the odds that anyone would remember a few kids who had written their names in the sidewalk twenty-something years ago?

The next house we came to was red brick with an inflatable pool in the yard. A few seconds after I rang the bell, a lady opened the door.

"Can I help you?" she asked. "Are you lost?"

She glanced back behind her as a little kid began to cry somewhere in the house.

"No," I said. "Um, I was wondering about something I saw written in the sidewalk on your street. A name? Ben?"

She stared blankly at me.

"I was wondering if maybe you knew who had written it there," I said. "It was probably done a long time ago."

She shook her head, wincing as the child let out a loud wail. "Sorry," she replied. "We just rent this place in the summers. Most of the houses on this street are rentals, too, I think."

"Oh," I sighed. "Well, thanks."

We turned to go.

"Wait," the woman said. "Try the pink house two doors down. The lady who lives there has been here forever. She might be able to help."

"Thanks a lot," I said. "We will."

"Good luck," she replied, shooting us a hurried smile as she closed the door.

We started toward the pink house. "Sammy, what if nobody remembers him?" I asked. "Then what?"

"I'm not sure," Sammy said, "but we'll figure something out."

The pink house was a shocking flamingo color. Wild vines bloomed around the porch, which was crowded with rocking chairs and wicker sofas so stuffed with pillows, I wasn't sure anyone could actually fit on them.

"Here goes nothing," I said, ringing the doorbell.

We waited for a few seconds before hearing someone shuffle to the door.

An ancient husk of a woman opened it, her whole body nodding from side to side like she was a passenger on a boat none of us could see. "Yes, dears?" she wheezed.

"Hi," I said. "Um, I was wondering if you could tell us about some kids who wrote their names in the sidewalk a long time ago? Clare, and Beth, and Ben?"

The woman blinked. "Beth," she said, looking at me as she sounded out the word. "Clare," she said, turning to Sammy. Then her face pulled back into a gaping smile. "Well, I never!"

Sammy and I exchanged a sidelong glance.

"Um, I'm Sammy," Sammy said. "And this is Miranda."

"Bah," said the old woman, waving Sammy's words away. "I would recognize the two of you anywhere, even if you have changed your hair. I'm glad to see you back together. Completely inseparable you were, all three of you. Where is Ben, anyhow?"

I felt my whole body go stiff as driftwood. Whoever this ancient woman was, she was trapped in a different era. An era when my mom and Aunt Clare were still joined at the hip, along with whoever Ben was.

"Um, I think you might be confused," Sammy said gently. "We're not—"

I interrupted her. "What else do you remember? About the three of us, I mean?"

"Oh, I remember more than people give me credit for," she said, lips cracking into a gummy grin. "I know it was you three who stole old Mr. Lemmon's hound dog, the one who kept half the town up every night. Found it a home on the mainland, did you? Good—that Lemmon was a wretched man. I won't soon forget the trouble you caused with the August Festival fireworks, either. I'm not sure Mrs. Freeman's left ear ever recovered."

I waited until she was done cackling. "And then, um, what happened?" I asked.

The smile on the old woman's face froze, then fell away.

"What happened," she repeated dully. "Yes . . . what happened on that island was a terrible thing."

"On the island?" Sammy said. "On Keeper's Island, you mean?"

"That's it," the old woman agreed. Then she looked up, and her cloudy eyes met mine. She found one of my hands and sandwiched it between her own. "It was a crying shame what happened on that island. I don't know how you ever survived it."

My heart thrashed like a fish caught on a line. *What happened to my mother on Keeper's Island?*

"What?" I gasped. "What did I survive?"

But before she could answer, the door opened wider, and another woman appeared.

"Betsy?" Sammy and I said in unison.

"Girls!" she said, stepping out onto the porch. She was wearing jeans and gardening gloves. "What are you doing here? Has Mama been talking your ear off?"

"Oh," Sammy breathed. "You live here?"

Betsy frowned, pushing a curly lock from her face. "Didn't y'all come to see me?"

"Yes," I said. "We did. We wanted to see if your mom was feeling better. We were actually just talking about my mom and Sammy's mom. And someone named Ben."

"Oh," Betsy said, her frown deepening. "Well, Mama's a tough old bird, but she does get confused sometimes. She probably needs a nap, don't you, Mama?"

The old woman blinked. "Can you take me home now?" she asked. "I still have all the children's presents to wrap before I get started with the dinner."

"See what I mean?" Betsy asked. "We'd better be getting in now. You two be careful in this heat."

"Wait," I said. "So did you know—"

"Sorry, Miranda," Betsy said. "I've got to get her in. But I'll see you soon, okay?"

Then she swept inside, shutting the door firmly behind her.

37

"*Um, what just happened?*" Sammy asked as we walked toward town to meet Caleb.

"I don't know," I said. My stomach felt funny, like one of Aunt Clare's pancakes being flipped up in the air.

"So we still don't know who Ben is," she mused. "But we *do* know that something definitely happened to your mom here."

"Not here," I said. "On Keeper's Island. And it was something really, really bad."

I don't know how you ever survived it. . . .

"Something bad enough that your mom never came back?" Sammy asked. "Bad enough that neither of our moms has ever mentioned this Ben person?"

"And bad enough that Betsy didn't want us to know either. She couldn't get us out of there fast enough."

"I noticed that, too. I guess Ben must have been their friend, huh? Or, like, a boyfriend or something?"

"Maybe," I said, wrinkling my nose. It was weird to think of Mom with a *boyfriend.* "But what could have happened between them that was so awful?"

As soon as we turned onto Oak Street, we saw Caleb running in our direction, weaving in and out of groups of tourists. He stopped when he got to the August Oak, clutching his side as he slumped onto our usual bench.

"You won't believe what just happened to us," Sammy said, as we sat down next to him.

"Me first," Caleb said, panting. "My dad found out who owns the island."

"And?" Sammy asked. "Who is it?"

Caleb leaned in closer, glancing around like he was afraid of being overheard. "Are you ready for this?" he asked.

"Just tell us, Caleb," I said.

"Okay. It's Mr. Taylor. Mr. Taylor owns Keeper's Island."

For just a moment, I forgot all about what Betsy's mom had said.

"Mr. Taylor?!" Sammy and I yelped. A couple of tourists glanced in our direction.

"You're sure?" I asked.

"I'm positive."

"I guess it makes sense," Sammy mused. "He must be pretty rich to have afforded that trip around the world."

"Well, I've been thinking about that," Caleb said. "According to the records my dad found, he bought the island just over ten years ago. Right before he set sail on the world's longest vacation."

"And?" Sammy prompted.

"*And* I was wondering . . . where did he get all the money to pay for that boat? To buy an *island*?"

"You think he found the treasure, don't you?" I asked. "You think it's real."

Caleb nodded. "It makes sense, doesn't it? He goes to the island and finds this treasure. But maybe he only finds some of it. So he buys the island and puts up Keep Out signs to make sure no one else will beat him to the rest. He cashes in what's left of the treasure to pay for his boat and all his travels. And then, when the money runs out—"

"—he comes back here," I breathed. "And he starts looking for the rest of it."

"It all fits," said Sammy. "That's why he didn't just tell us he owned it when I was asking him about the island. What he's doing is probably illegal, huh? Shouldn't treasure like that be in a museum or something? And if he found it before he bought the island, it definitely didn't belong to him."

My head had begun to spin. It was all too much. But what Caleb was saying didn't feel right.

"You guys," I said, "this is *Mr. Taylor* we're talking about. I mean, he's just a really nice old man. Isn't he? He could have gotten us in a lot of trouble, but he didn't. I don't think he would do something that was against the law. He wouldn't steal."

Even as I said it, a tiny part of me began to wonder. All those beautiful things he'd brought back—had he been honest with us about where he'd gotten them? What if he'd stolen them like he'd stolen treasure from Keeper's Island?

"If there's one thing you learn as a journalist," Sammy said sagely, "it's that people are capable of anything. Even the ones you think you know."

"Do you have a better theory?" Caleb asked me. "I mean, if he didn't have anything to hide, why wouldn't he just tell us that he owned the island? Why is he making secret trips out there at night?"

"If it *is* him out there," I said.

"Come on." Sammy stood up. "We need to grab our stuff from the beach and get home before Mom comes out to check on us."

We filled Caleb in about Betsy's mom as we walked. We must have been late, because Jai was already gone from the tower, his shift over. We grabbed our towels and strode faster.

"What did Betsy's mom mean about Keeper's Island?" Caleb asked as we walked up Sammy's porch steps.

"I'm not sure," Sammy said, flopping into a hammock. "But if Betsy hadn't shown up right then, we might know by now."

"We were so close," I murmured.

"Mr. Taylor, Betsy, Keeper's Island, Miranda's family, Ben, and my mom," Sammy mused, "they're all connected."

"But no one will tell us the truth about them," Caleb said, sitting down in one of the rocking chairs.

"The only person willing to tell the truth has probably already forgotten it again," I said bitterly. "And I'm leaving in just a few days."

"Which is why we can't waste any more time," Sammy said.

"What do you mean?" asked Caleb.

"I mean we have to find out what happened to Miranda's mom on that island. And if no one will tell us what it was, then we're just going to have to go there and find out for ourselves."

"Are you serious?" I asked.

Caleb nodded solemnly. "I'm in."

"But how? When?"

"Tomorrow," Sammy said. "It's perfect. Everyone will be at the park for the festival. They'll be distracted. Nobody will notice if we slip away for a few hours. We'll get to the harbor, borrow a boat, and sail it out to the island."

"Even if we did all that," I protested, "what are we expecting to find when we get there?"

"Answers," said Caleb simply.

"Maybe there will be some clues," Sammy said. "Something that will help us figure out what happened to your mom." She paused. "But it's really up to you, Miranda. It's your family. And we know you don't like water, so if you don't think you can handle it, it's okay."

"I—" I started.

Before I could say anything, we all turned at the sound of a floorboard creaking.

Jai stood in the doorway. His eyebrows cast dark shadows over his face.

"Sorry," he said. "Couldn't help but overhear."

38

Sammy jumped up like she'd been bitten by something. "Jai!" she yelped.

Jai's eyes fell on me for a moment, and his frown deepened. "You're late. Lucky for you Mom's not home yet."

"Well, this is none of your business," Sammy said. "So just go text one of your girlfriends or something."

"Funny story," he said. "One of them *did* text me. Something about you and Miranda knocking on people's doors and asking about someone named Ben. You said you were helping Caleb and his dad. You lied to me."

"Just go away," Sammy demanded.

"I'm not going anywhere, and neither are you three. Especially not to that island."

Sammy stomped her foot. "You don't understand anything, Jai! We *have* to. Please just go inside and pretend you didn't hear."

To my surprise, Jai didn't get mad or say something mean. Instead he just shook his head and sighed. He glanced at me again. "I'm sorry," he said. "No can do."

Sammy's chin began to dimple. "Are you going to tell Mom?"

He hesitated. "No," he said. "But I'll be watching you three tomorrow. And if you take so much as a step toward the harbor, then I *will* tell. And she'll ground you for life. No more sailing lessons, no more school paper. She'll never let you out of the house again. Got it?"

Sammy's face had screwed up into a furious knot. "Fine," she said. "But I'm never, ever going to forgive you."

Jai shrugged. "That's up to you."

He disappeared back into the house, and a few seconds later we heard him plucking out a song on his guitar.

"So are we going to listen to him?" Caleb said.

"No way," Sammy replied. "We're going. I don't know how, but—"

"No," I said flatly. "We're not."

They stared at me.

"I can't let you guys get in trouble for me," I said, my voice shaking. "I know how important the school paper is to you, Sammy. I can't let you get grounded from it. You'll find another story to write. And your family has been so nice to me this whole summer. I don't want you lying to them for me anymore."

"But—" Sammy started.

"Look, didn't you ever think maybe there's a reason nobody wants me to know the truth? Maybe it's just too terrible. Maybe I'm better off not knowing."

I had promised myself not to run from Mom's secret, but that was before we'd talked to Betsy's mom. I kept seeing her in my head, watching the smile falling from her face to reveal a dark shadow underneath.

I don't know how you ever survived it. . . .

And then there was that strange feeling I had gotten the first time I ever looked at Keeper's Island. A creeping dread. Maybe it had been a warning.

"Miranda—" Caleb tried.

I stood up. "I'm going in. I need to get started on my piecrust for the festival tomorrow."

And before either of them could object, I whisked through the door, letting it slam shut behind me.

The next morning, I woke up with a churning stomach and a bad headache. I had barely slept at all the night before. Every time I almost fell asleep, a new voice would shake me awake.

It was a crying shame what happened on that island. . . .

Oftentimes the past is the best place to look when we need help understanding something in our present. . . .

I do think she's saddled us with quite a big burden here.

Please don't forget me.

Please come home.

When I finally did fall asleep, it was just to wake up

again, gasping for air. My drowning dream had come back.

MOMMY!

Daylight burned through the windows. I threw my blanket off and looked over at Sammy's bed. It was empty. We didn't have sailing lessons that day since it was festival day, so nobody had woken me up. The clock on Sammy's bedside table said it was 10:03.

When I stumbled downstairs, the Grovers were sitting around the table eating waffles. For a moment, I stood on the landing above and watched them. Uncle Amar was reading the paper while Aunt Clare rubbed the back of his head. She was talking to Sammy about the festival while Jai poured half a bottle of syrup onto his waffle stack. Sammy said something that made Aunt Clare laugh, and suddenly I almost wished I had never come to August Isle in the first place.

It wasn't fair to know that families as great as the Grovers existed when you weren't actually a part of one.

The weight of dread that had been growing in my stomach felt like an iron anchor, threatening to drag me down, down, down.

Uncle Amar spotted me as he turned the page of his paper. "Ah," he said, "there she is! The lady of the hour!"

"Oh, good!" Aunt Clare said. "I was going to send

Sammy up for you soon. You better get those pies in the oven so we can head over to the festival as soon as they're ready. Come have some breakfast first."

"Actually, I'm not really hungry," I said.

"You don't feel well?" she asked.

I shook my head.

"I hope you aren't coming down with something," Aunt Clare said, pushing back her chair and getting up. As I shuffled down the rest of the stairs, she reached out to feel my forehead. I closed my eyes as her cool hand pressed reassuringly against my skin.

"No fever," she said.

"There *is* something going around the isle," Uncle Amar said. "A bad cold."

Sammy was shooting me a meaningful look. She knew why I felt so horrible, and that it had nothing to do with a cold.

"Well, you don't have to make the pies if you don't feel up to it," Aunt Clare said.

I was supposed to make two pies: one for the competition and one for us to eat ourselves afterward. I would rather have gone back to bed and pulled the covers up over my head. But I could hear the disappointment in Aunt Clare's voice, and I thought of all the time she had spent helping me practice. I couldn't let her down now.

"No," I said, "it's okay. I want to. But maybe—could

I stay home instead of going with you to the festival?"

Jai's head whipped around toward me. Sammy's eyebrows shot up in a question, but I gave my head the tiniest shake. They both probably thought I was planning some kind of escape to Keeper's Island. Really, I just didn't want to spend the day watching all the happy families go on carnival rides and eat hot dogs and play silly games together. I couldn't bear the Grovers being so nice to me, treating me like I belonged with them, when I was just going to leave in two days.

It was better to pretend I was already gone.

"Well, I suppose," Aunt Clare said uncertainly. "Amar can stay with you if you don't want to come."

"No," I protested. "I'll be fine. Really."

"Are you kidding?" Uncle Amar said. "An excuse to stay home and put my feet up instead of going to that circus? You're an angel, Miranda."

"Then it's settled," Aunt Clare said. "Amar will be here if you start feeling any worse. Sammy and I will take your pie and enter it for you. Won't we, Sammy?"

I set to work on my pies, rolling out the thoroughly chilled crusts and making the lemon curds.

It was actually a relief how quiet my head got while I worked. Almost peaceful. As I put the pies into the oven, I promised myself that I was going to keep baking when I got home. I would teach myself to make cakes next. They would be easy after learning pies. I would make pound cakes and layer cakes and cheese-cakes and cupcakes. At least that way I could hold on to one tiny bit of my summer here.

When the pies were cooling, Sammy and I went back upstairs, where she was supposed to be getting ready for the festival. Instead she grabbed Bluey and cuddled him between her arms.

"I want to stay here with you," she said, pouting. "The festival won't be any fun on my own."

Bluey's one eye looked at me accusingly.

"You won't be on your own," I said. "Caleb will be there."

"I know you aren't sick. You're just sad. That's why I should stay with you."

"Honestly, Sammy," I said, "I really just want to be alone. I need to—"

"What?"

"Nothing," I muttered, biting my lip. I had been about to say *I need to get used to it again*. But I didn't want to make Sammy feel worse for me than she already did.

A few minutes later, Jai appeared in the doorway.

"What are you doing here, creep?" Sammy snapped, glaring at him.

"I want to talk to Miranda," he said.

"I'm not trying to get to Keeper's Island, Jai," I said.

He crossed his arms over his chest and shot me a searching look. Sammy might be mad at him, but I wasn't. I could see he wasn't being a jerk. He just didn't want his little sister sailing out in the ocean on her own. Deep down, he really cared about Sammy.

"Do you promise?" he asked.

"Promise."

Uncle Amar forced me to eat some lunch, and then Aunt Clare, Sammy, and Jai finally left. I waved good-bye, then went back upstairs to lie down. I must have been pretty tired from the night before, because the next thing I knew, I was waking up to the sound of my phone bleeping.

It was a message from Dad.

Good luck at the festival today, kiddo!

Still nothing from Mom.

Sitting up and looking around Sammy's room for something to do, I decided that even though I wasn't leaving for another two days, I might as well start packing. My stuff had gotten strewn all over the place, and besides, I knew it would make Sammy sad to see me pack.

With nothing else to keep me occupied, I took my time drifting back and forth across the room. I found two of my tank tops in her dresser, my sunglasses in her laundry hamper, and my headphones stuffed into a mug of pencils on top of her bookshelf. When I had collected all my things I could see, I lay on my stomach on Sammy's bed and swung my head down to look under it. There was a single sandal, a potato-chip bag, and a book.

I pulled out the sandal and the book. The sandal was one of mine—it had been missing since my first week in August Isle—but the picture book, I saw, was the one Caleb had brought back from the library. He had given it to Sammy, and she must have thrown it onto her bed, where it had dropped down in the crack between the mattress and the wall.

I stared at the cover. I hadn't really looked at it before. On it, a starfish was peeking out from behind a sprig of seaweed, looking scared, like maybe it was hiding from something. The book was called *Cecil the Starfish Gets Lost*.

I felt a rustle of recognition deep in my chest. I flipped through the pages. It was about a little starfish who gets separated from his mother in a tide pool. He's nearly stung by a stingray, eaten by a shark, and stabbed by a blowfish, but just when he's about to give up, his mother finds him again.

I saw why the librarian didn't want the book. Some of the pages were stuck together, and there were marker stains on others. The paper was worn so soft, it felt like cloth.

Someone had read this book many, many times.

It seemed like kind of a strange thing for Mr. Taylor to have. Why would he own a book like this unless he had once had a child to read it to?

I thought back to the way he'd looked after he had told us the story about Illari falling from the stars. How he had been so sad. I had known then, deep down, that he had lost someone. But I had never thought that it might be a child.

When I turned to the last page—a full illustration of Cecil's mom tucking him into his seaweed bed—I was sure that I had read the book before. Something about the colors the illustrator had used for the seaweed— deep blues and greens—made me feel comfortable and safe, like I was three years old again and being tucked into bed by my own mom.

I turned the last page to reveal the inside back cover. As I did, something fell out. A picture.

It showed a man on a mellow gold beach, bending down over a tiny kid in overalls who was stumbling through the sand.

The man in the photo was Mr. Taylor, though it took me a few seconds of staring to see it. He had more hair on top of his head and no beard, but it was definitely him.

As my eyes fell on the tiny kid he was hunched over, my heart came to a grinding halt.

The child peered up at the camera with a mischievous smile. One of its hands was enveloped in Mr. Taylor's.

The other was clutching the flipper of a stuffed blue dolphin.

A dolphin that was missing one eye.

When my heart finally began beating again, all the blood seemed to rush into my head, where I could hear it pounding.

Minutes passed by as I stared at the picture, blinking, squinting. Trying to make sure that what I thought I was seeing was real. I even held Bluey up next to the picture to compare them. The dolphin in the photo was identical.

Which meant that the kid in the picture had to be . . . *me*.

"Why am I in a picture with Mr. Taylor?" I murmured aloud.

The answer was right there, staring me in the face.

It might as well have been painted in big bold letters across Sammy's wall. *I* was Mr. Taylor's family. That was the reason he had never talked about them. He must know who I was. He had known since Sammy had called my name on the night I broke into his house.

That was probably the only reason he hadn't turned us in to the police. Instead, he had told us to come back. So he could get to know his granddaughter.

Because for some reason, Mom had kept us apart. She had lied to me about him dying in a car crash.

Mr. Taylor wasn't just some nice old man with interesting stories.

"He's my grandfather," I whispered aloud. Saying the words made me even more certain they were true. They had to be. What else could explain the picture?

I felt a momentary surge of joy so intense, it made me shiver. I had another grandfather. And he was the one person in the world I would pick to be my grandfather if I could.

But then the questions came.

Was *this* the secret Mom was keeping from me? But why? And why hadn't *Mr. Taylor* told me the truth?

Surely he would tell me now. Now that I knew who he was.

I wasn't going to give him any other choice.

I sprang out of bed and headed for the door, tucking the picture into my pocket.

I could hear the TV playing, and Uncle Amar snoring over it. How long had he been asleep?

I bit my lip. I knew I shouldn't leave. What if Uncle Amar woke up and found me gone? It would be much better just to wait until tomorrow afternoon to go see Mr. Taylor.

Except that I couldn't. I couldn't wait a whole day to find out if he really was my grandfather.

I won't be gone long, I told myself. *Uncle Amar will never even know.*

Then, before I could talk myself out of it, I was slipping through the front door and onto the porch.

Music and laughter floated over the Isle like a cotton-candy cloud as I ran the distance to Mr. Taylor's house, but the streets were deserted. Everyone was at the festival.

Mr. Taylor wouldn't be there, though. He had told us so.

I broke into a sprint when his house came into view, racing down the path and up onto the porch stairs. I pounded against the door and waited, panting.

There was no answer. Nothing stirred inside the house.

My fingers hovered above the door handle for a second before pressing it down and pushing.

Just like it had the first night, the door swung right open.

The house was dim inside.

"Hello?" I called. "Mr. Taylor?"

I walked into the living room. No Mr. Taylor there or in the dining room. I tried the library next, but there was no sign of him there either. And it wasn't just Mr. Taylor who was missing. Safira wasn't in her cage, and Slug wasn't in his usual spot on the living-room rug.

Why would Mr. Taylor take Slug and Safira with him, unless he was going to be gone a long time?

The house felt different now that I was sure there was no one here. The silence was eerie, and I wanted to leave, just like I had wanted to the night I broke in. But I made myself keep going, through the library and into the kitchen. If Mr. Taylor had left any clue as to where he had gone, I had to find it. I needed to see him, maybe more than I had ever needed to do anything in my life.

The kitchen was tidy but old-fashioned. No dishes sat in the sink, no leftovers on the stove. I glanced at the ancient refrigerator, but it was a blank canvas. No birthday cards or appointment reminders.

In the opposite corner of the room was a simple wooden table with four chairs around it. I wondered how long it had been since the chairs had had people to fill them. Then, with a start, I wondered if *I* had ever sat at this kitchen table. Maybe as a baby on my grandfather's lap.

I ran my hands over its grooves, like I might be able to feel my chubby baby hand reaching out to me from the past, doing the exact same thing.

As I stared down, wondering about every scratch and scar in the wood, something else caught my eye. Some kind of markings on the wall behind the table.

When I peered closer, I saw that they were little red horizontal lines. Next to each line, a label had been scrawled.

"Miranda, 1 year, 29 inches," read the line closest to the floor.

I let out a little gasp. It sounded loud in the silent house. My fingers traced my name on the wall, then the red lines as they moved up. One for every six months until I turned three (39 inches). Then they stopped.

So I *had* been in this house before this summer. But not since I was three years old. Too young to remember it, even.

Just as I was straightening my knees to stand, my gaze landed on the other wall that came together to form the corner behind the table. And I froze.

There was another height chart drawn onto that wall, this one in blue.

The lines on the second chart went higher than mine, so I barely had to bend to see what was written next to the top line.

"Matthew, 7 years, 47 inches."

For the second time in an hour, my heart seemed to stop beating. I forced out a breath that shook my whole body. I closed my eyes and opened them. The name was still there.

"I don't understand," I said aloud. "Who is Matthew?"

But the empty house returned no answer.

41

I was not the only child who had been in this house, whose height had been lovingly recorded on this wall.

There was someone else, a boy, who my grandfather had loved for seven whole years.

"Matthew," I whispered, the name trembling through my lips.

I didn't know any Matthews, and yet the name rang some distant bell, the same way the picture book had done. Had I known him? Was he Mr. Taylor's grandchild, too? That would make him my cousin. Or a brother who had somehow been hidden from me my whole life. I dismissed that thought. Even after everything I had learned, I couldn't believe that Mom and Dad would keep something like that from me.

But if I had a cousin, Mom *must* have lied to me about her being an only child.

Why, though? I wondered desperately. Why would she lie to me about so much? And what did it all have to do with Ben and Keeper's Island?

I looked back at the highest marking on the wall. It came up to my shoulder. Seven years. Matthew had been seven years old when the last mark was made.

Either Matthew had stopped coming to this house after he turned seven, or he had never gotten any older.

My gaze lingered on the name for one last second. Then I turned and ran, only stopping when I was safely out on the porch. I slumped down onto the bottom step, where I tried to make myself take deep breaths.

"Are you all right, dear?"

I snapped my head up to see a woman standing over me. I recognized her as the woman who lived next door. She was wearing a bathrobe and slippers and held out a glass of water. "I saw you from my window," she said in a nasal voice. "You're shivering. Looks like you've come down with the same thing I have."

I took the water gratefully and drank it down in a couple of gulps. "Thanks," I croaked.

"You're one of the kids who's been helping over

here, aren't you?" she said, eyeing me curiously. "I've seen you from my window."

"Yeah."

"Well, I'm glad. This place has been such a mess for so long. I tried to get the town to condemn it so it would get torn down, but they wouldn't do it. Of course, now that Taylor's back, I have to deal with the noise. That bird is like an ambulance siren at night."

"Do you know where he is?" I asked.

"He left here just a little while ago," the woman said, sniffling. "Looked like he was headed for the harbor. He probably wanted to watch the fireworks from his boat. It *is* nicer that way—you don't have to fight the crowd. Though I'm not sure why he had to take so much stuff."

"Stuff?" I asked, stiffening. "What stuff?"

She frowned at me. "Well, I didn't ask. It's not really my business what was in all those crates. Although whatever it was, it was heavy, because he had a job lifting them into his truck. I watched him haul things back and forth for a good ten minutes. Do you need me to call someone for you, dear? You really don't look well."

"No," I said. "I'm fine." I stood up and shoved the water glass back into her hands. "Thanks a lot."

I started off, then stopped. "Actually, you said . . . you said the man who lives here is named Taylor?"

It had just occurred to me that if Mr. Taylor was my grandfather, he must have lied to us about his name. Mom's maiden name was—

"Crawford," the woman said, at the very same time I thought it. "His name is Taylor Crawford."

She was looking at me funny now, saying words I wasn't listening to. All I could hear was the name Crawford echoing in my head. So it was true, then. Mr. Taylor was my grandfather. And he hadn't lied about his name. Not exactly.

I started off again, running for the harbor.

If he was just going to watch fireworks in his boat, why would he have packed so much stuff? Why would he have taken Slug and Safira?

Maybe he was headed for Keeper's Island.

Or maybe leaving runs in the family, said a voice in my head.

He wouldn't do that, I thought. *Would he?*

Then again, what if Sammy and Caleb had been right about him? What if he wasn't the person I thought he was, and he *had* just come home to find the rest of the treasure? And now that he'd found it, he was taking off again?

I had to catch him before he set sail.

I tore down Oak Street, past the August Oak, its leaves rustling in the breeze like hands clapping me on, and past the darkened shops with Closed signs hanging on their doors. I didn't stop when I felt a cramp biting into my side. I only slowed down enough to wriggle my phone from my pocket.

I started typing a text to Sammy and Caleb.

MEET ME AT THE HARBOR ASAP—HAVE TO

But before I could finish, I felt myself go flying as I shot my hands out to break my fall. I had stumbled over the same square of sidewalk I had tripped on before.

I could tell right away from the sting that I had scraped my knee really bad. Sure enough, when I stood up again, pricks of blood were beginning to appear all over it. My phone was lying a few feet away, the screen cracked into about a thousand slivers. When I tapped it, nothing happened. The phone was dead.

I said a word I wasn't supposed to say, then tucked what was left of the phone back into my pocket and started running again, pushing myself faster and faster. Finally the bridge over the harbor came into view. I hurled myself toward it, only stopping when I reached the guardrail.

Then I stood, gasping for breath, looking out at the harbor. A large sailboat was just about to cross into the open water. It was hard to tell at first with twilight settling down on the Isle, but I could just make out the word "Albatross" painted on its side.

My grandfather was already gone.

I began to panic. What if he *was* leaving for another ten years? Or even for good this time?

"Wait!" I bellowed. "Please, don't go! COME BACK!"

But I knew he couldn't hear me. All he would be able to hear was the sound of waves crashing into the hull of his boat.

I dropped my face, dripping with sweat, into my palms and let out a sob.

He was gone, and I was alone.

Unless . . .

When I let my palms slide from my face, I found myself looking straight down at the sailing beach.

Three little sailboats were just sitting there, bobbing merrily in the water.

Could I do it? Could I sail after his boat all on my own? Small boats could be faster than larger ones, I knew. And Mr. Taylor didn't have *that* much of a head start.

Jason had been a good teacher. I knew I *could* sail after Mr. Taylor. I just didn't know if I was brave enough to actually do it. Even looking at the water was making my throat feel like it was about to close up.

Right then, the wind began to blow, tangling through my hair and whisking it toward the ocean.

And I remembered how Mr. Taylor had told me that family was the most important thing of all.

Even more important than fear.

After all, what good was being brave if you weren't brave when it really counted?

I took a last deep breath. Then I was sprinting down to the beach, stuffing my arms through a life jacket, and unclipping a boat from its line.

"I am Miranda," I whispered as I pushed it away from the beach, "brave and bold. I am Miranda, brave and bold." I kept going until I was splashing waist deep in the water.

Then I hauled myself up onto the boat, unfurled the sail, and headed for the open sea.

42

My toes clung to the slick plastic as I moved around the boat, putting in the daggerboard and securing the sheets. Salt water stung my scraped knee, which was still bleeding.

When I was done, I pulled my life jacket so tight, I couldn't breathe. I loosened it again, but only a bit.

As the boat glided out of the bay and into the open water, a scream rose up from the back of my throat. The sound of it was drowned out by the first wave charging into the prow. I held tight to the mast, sure that the surge would capsize the boat and send me flying into the water. But the boat merely bobbed up and down as it plowed on.

After that, my breath became steadier, and I pulled the sail tighter, urging the little boat on faster.

I looked back at August Isle then. A wreath of rosy lights around the Ferris wheel blinked to life as I watched, and I could just catch the sound of a giddy scream and a few cheerful notes of music over the hum of the ocean.

If something happened to the boat and I fell into the water, would someone hear my cries and come save me? Or would I just float until I couldn't float any longer? Or until . . .

Images of man-eating sharks filled my head.

I pushed them away, instead imagining my guardian sea turtle pedaling her flippers below my boat, keeping watch over me, ready to swim me to safety if I fell in.

I did not look back again.

I felt the first bit of hope when I began to gain on Mr. Taylor. Every couple of minutes, I would realize that his boat had gotten bigger. Closer.

But then I lost sight of it as it sailed around the far side of Keeper's Island. Was he stopping? Or sailing out to sea? It was one thing to sail from August Isle to Keeper's Island. It was another to chase Mr. Taylor out into the endless horizon. If I couldn't catch him before he passed the island, I would have to turn back.

As I rounded Keeper's Island, I saw the Keep Out

signs Jason had told us about, posted in the water all around it. I squinted at the island through the last scraps of daylight. The trees were ghostly shadows, the beach a gloomy stretch of gray.

The hairs on my neck stood up. I felt as though my heart was an alarm bell, pulsing a warning through my chest.

I tore my gaze away and looked ahead, where a long wooden dock poked out into the water. Miraculously, Mr. Taylor's boat was bobbing at the end of it. Relief swept through me.

Soon, I had steered my boat close enough to reach out and grab the dock.

I lifted myself up, and for just a moment, I let myself sit there, savoring the wood planks, dry and sturdy. I had sailed by myself from August Isle to Keeper's Island. And I hadn't drowned.

Any other time, I might have felt so proud of myself, I could burst.

But now I stood up, tied my boat to the moorings on the dock, and looked around uncertainly. I unclipped my life jacket and let it fall to my feet.

"Mr. Taylor?" I called. Even though I knew he was my grandfather, it felt weird to call him anything else.

There was no answer. His boat looked empty.

I set off toward the beach.

I walked slowly, because with every step I took, my

dread seemed to grow. My eyes scanned the island. I could see the silhouette of the lighthouse looming over the trees beyond the beach. It looked like there was something else—some kind of hut—next to it, like a dog crouched next to its owner.

Once I found myself standing on the sand, still warm from the day's sun, I stopped. With a shiver, I remembered the story of the lighthouse keeper's ghost. A trembling started in my heart and rippled out to my fingers and my toes.

"Mr. Taylor?" I called again, louder this time. "Mr. Taylor? It's Miranda!"

When there was still no answer, I forced myself to keep walking, toward the trees.

A sudden sound turned my head. A nearby clump of low palms began to rustle. I squinted, but I still couldn't see what was making them move.

"Mr. Taylor?" I called. My voice trembled now, too. "Is that you?"

For a second, all was still. Then something emerged from the palms. Something that looked like a cloaked figure with its arms outstretched. Something that moved like no human I had ever seen. Something that began to shriek as it rushed toward me.

I tried to scream, but the sound lodged in my throat. I found myself running back, back the way I had come. Except—where was the dock? I had run at a diagonal, and now it was too far to reach. If I wanted to escape, there was only one place to go.

I hesitated for a single second. Then I darted straight into the surf. My scream finally found its way up, and as I ran into the black ocean, the sound of it filled the night.

I kept running until I was knee-deep in the water. Then my legs crumpled.

Someone was pulling me, gripping my calves, tugging me out to sea.

"No!" I cried. "Help!"

A wave crashed over my head, filling my nose and mouth with seawater. My arms thrashed, my feet kicked, but I couldn't seem to find my way to the surface.

It kept getting farther away, and soon I felt myself growing tired. It was hard to make my limbs do what I wanted them to.

After a while, they went still.

For a long moment, I found myself cocooned in darkness. I somehow sensed that I was alone. Whatever had pulled me out into the water was gone now.

A strange thought appeared in my mind.

Wasn't there something I was supposed to remember? Hadn't I been trying to find something?

The vision came to me from nowhere. A perfect starfish lying in the surf. *I want that,* I thought. *It's just like Cecil in the book!*

Don't go into the waves, Miranda, said a voice. A boy's voice. But whose?

I was drifting, I realized. My thoughts were drifting. They weren't making any sense. I needed to stay alert. To fight.

But my lungs were burning, and I was already drifting again. Back, back, back . . .

My hands shoot out through the water, but which way is up and which way is down?

In my dream, it isn't dark. It's daytime, and I am pushing toward the light of the sun. I break through the surface, gasping for air.

"MOMMY!" I bellow.

Another wave overtakes me, swallowing me, gobbling me up in its frothy jaws. My chest feels like fireworks. I am weaker now. My eyes are closing. I am going to fall down, down, down to the bottom of the ocean.

But then the current tumbles me up for a brief moment, lifting me almost to the water's surface.

It's my last chance, I know. I shoot an arm up out of the water.

And someone takes hold.

I am being pulled up, up, up.

The first breath is like coming back to life. I cough, choking on water as I try to take a second, and open my eyes to see my rescuer.

Not Mommy.

A man.

His name comes to me.

Uncle.

My uncle's cheeks are red, his eyes screwed up with the effort of freeing me from the current. He is shouting at me to hold on, so I do.

I cling to his neck. I look over his shoulders to see another wave heading toward us, baring its thousand white fangs. He looks back and sees it, tells me to hold on tighter.

But he doesn't see what's out there beyond the wave. He doesn't see the boy floundering in the blue, blue, blue.

I tug at my uncle's shoulder. I have to make him see. He's going the wrong way. I start to yell the boy's name—but the ferocious wave has reached us now, and the last thing I know is that I am being swallowed by a monster. And then . . . and then . . .

I felt a strong hand take hold of mine, raking me through the water, yanking me up so fiercely that a searing pain shot through my elbow.

I was suddenly free from the ocean's clutches, gasping for breath. Someone was holding me, someone with a scratchy beard, and I was clinging to his neck as we waded back to the dark beach.

Except we were going the wrong way. Because Matthew was still out there in the waves, wasn't he?

But that's not what I called him, was it? Everyone else called him Matty, but I couldn't quite manage the M sound, so when I said it, it came out "Batty."

He had eyes like Mom's; I remember that. Blue-gray, like the sea, like the color of something that's always slipping through your hands.

Wasn't I always trying to catch him? Wasn't he always running just out of arm's reach?

"Wait for me, Batty!"

A little scar above his ear. A telescope, the color green, a jar of fireflies. *When I grow up, I'm going to be an astronaut.* That was all I remembered about the boy who had gone into the sea.

"Wait," I sputtered. "Stop. Batty—Matty—he's still out there!"

When we didn't stop, I began to flail against the man carrying me. "You're going the wrong way!" I cried. "We have to go back for Matty!"

"No, Miranda," said the man gently. "Matty's not out there."

And I realized that he was right. It was nighttime now, not day, and it was Mr. Taylor carrying me, not my uncle. I could hear a dog barking from shore. I was not the little girl I had been a moment ago. I was all tangled up in memories—ones I didn't even know I had—like a fish squirming in a net.

Time was moving in strange lurches, and when I opened my eyes next, I was lying on the sand, looking up at a heavy sky of stars. Mr. Taylor was staring down at me, his eyes wide with panic, the light of the moon like a halo around his head.

"You're my grandfather," I said groggily.

He breathed a sigh of relief. "I am," he replied.

"And I have an uncle? So Matty is my cousin?"

My grandfather nodded.

"What happened to them? Where's Matty?"

He brought a clenched fist to his mouth and made a strange, wounded sound. "He's gone, Miranda. Matty's been gone a long time."

"But I just found him," I murmured. Then my stomach gave a violent twist, and I turned on my side and sputtered out more seawater as my grandfather gently stroked my hair.

44

When I could finally stop coughing, I sat up. The motion sent pain radiating from my elbow. My lungs felt like they were smoldering. Mr. Taylor had tied some kind of cloth around my knee to stop it from bleeding, but it still throbbed.

My grandfather sat next to me on the sand, face grave, beard dripping seawater. On his other side, Slug stared at me, thumping his tail twice when my eyes met his. Mr. Taylor handed me a canteen of water, and I drank.

"There was something," I gasped, suddenly remembering why I had gone into the water in the first place. "Something chasing me."

"Safira," Mr. Taylor said, pointing back up toward the trees. "It was just Safira. She can be very intimidating when she has her wings fully stretched."

Had I really almost drowned running away from Safira? Could the cloaked arms I saw reaching for me have simply been her wings?

"But the thing . . . it was screaming."

"Yes, she gets restless around sundown, and then she can be quite loud. That's why I like to bring her out here with me. Give her a chance to stretch her wings. I'm very sorry she frightened you."

I remembered then what Mr. Taylor's neighbor had said about Safira screaming like an ambulance. That kind of scream would be loud enough to carry across the water, all the way back to the Isle. So it was Safira I'd been hearing all along. At another time, this might have struck me as funny.

"We should get you back to the Isle," said Mr. Taylor.

"No!" I cried. "Please—I'm tired of waiting. I need to know what happened. I was on this island before, wasn't I? And I got caught up in the current. I always thought it was a dream, but it wasn't. It was a memory."

"Yes," said Mr. Taylor. "It was. We never did find out how you ended up in the surf."

"There was a starfish," I said. "I was just trying to get it."

"Ah," breathed Mr. Taylor. "A starfish. Your uncle Ben saw you go running into the surf and—"

My mind was spinning in every direction all at once. Ben wasn't Mom's friend. He was her brother.

"What happened to him?"

The moon traced a grimace on Mr. Taylor's face. He reached for Slug and gripped his fur in one hand. Then he closed his eyes and sighed. "Perhaps," he said, "we should start at the beginning."

Finally, Mr. Taylor was going to tell me his story.

Finally, someone was going to tell me the truth.

45

Once, there was a young man who lived with his beautiful wife and two perfect children. Above all else, the man cared for his family. He himself had been poor as a boy, and he vowed that he would make a good life for his wife and children, that they would never want for anything. And in this he succeeded beyond his wildest dreams.

But as his youth fell away from him, a change came over the man's heart. Above all else, he cared for success and power. Always he thirsted for more. He spent most of his time away from his family and bought them beautiful things to make up for his absence: among them a grand sailboat and a great house by the sea.

But these gifts made a poor substitute for a father and a husband.

The years passed in this way, and one day, a knock came upon the door. A policeman told the man that his wife had been killed in a car accident. His children had long since grown up, and now the man was left alone. Then all the power in the world could not have eased his sorrow.

He begged his children's forgiveness and vowed upon his wife's grave that he would return to the man he had been long ago, who cared for his family above all else.

By that time, his son had become a father himself, to a little boy who started coming often to stay in the house by the sea. The man was proud of his grandson, who anyone could see had a hungry mind. He bought the boy a telescope, and he and his grandson spent hours looking up into the vast night sky together, pondering the mysteries of the universe.

When the little boy grew sleepy, he would ask his grandfather to tell him a story. But the man knew none, for he had been too busy in life to notice things so silly as stories. He bought his grandson books to read instead.

Next, a granddaughter was born, this time to the man's daughter, who he knew had never quite managed to forgive him. Again, the man was proud of the girl, who anyone could see had a loyal heart. She watched the world with wide, quiet eyes, and she chased after her cousin with chubby outstretched hands.

One afternoon, the man took his son and his grandchildren for a ride on his sailboat to a small island where they would explore and picnic until the sun went down and the stars came out. Then they would climb into the old lighthouse, peer up at the sky through the boy's telescope, and count their lucky stars.

As they walked, the man's phone began to ring. You see, though he had vowed not to make the same mistakes any longer, he was never able to give up his work completely. Though he had money enough to last several lifetimes, deep in his heart he sometimes still craved the power he had once known.

So, thinking he would be only a moment, the man turned away from his family to talk to a woman of great importance.

But by the time the first scream shattered the calm afternoon, the man was already on the far side of the beach.

The little girl, he saw, had been swept up into the current, and his son was rushing after her. By the time the man had sprinted the length of the beach, his son was crouching over the girl in the sand, where she soon began to sputter and cough.

"Thank God," said the man's son. "Thank God she's all right."

But the man was hardly listening. Because the little girl sat up now, and she pointed to the water.

"Batty," she sputtered. "Batty followed Uncle into waves."

The two men followed her pointing finger, and then the younger began to run once more. When he met the waves, he began to swim. After he met the shape of his son bobbing in the water, he tried to turn back, but the current only pushed them farther from shore.

The older man scooped the little girl up and ran across the sand to his boat. They sailed back and forth across the waves, searching for the lost boys. Soon more boats arrived to help. One came to take the little girl back to her mother.

Once more, the man found himself alone. He sailed on and on, until his hope dwindled away, until darkness fell. And still he sailed. He bellowed curses at the stars. He fell on his knees and wept. He sailed until, unbearably, the sun rose again in the sky.

Even when he understood at last that his son and grandson had been swallowed by the sea, he continued to sail. Until one day, he decided to sail away.

Why had he taken the phone call? Why had he broken his promise to his family? He no longer deserved the family he had left, and he could no longer bear to live in the house by the sea.

The farther he sailed, the harder he tried to forget. He lost himself in new places, traveling by sea and over land, wishing to become a man with no memory. A man of no stories.

Then one winter night, many months later, he lay on the deck of his boat, bobbing in the waves of a distant sea. And as he stared up at the stars, one of them whispered to him with a voice like a bell.

"Please don't forget me."

The man began to tremble, for he knew the voice he had heard. And he knew then that he had been wrong to try to forget his sorrows. Instead of forgetting, he would make sure his lost boys were remembered.

He would tell everyone he met about the little boy who loved stars and stories, and the father who gave his life for his son, and the man who had turned his back on them both. In return, he would ask for stories that needed remembering, to add to his collection.

And so he became a man of a thousand stories. Stories that he wished to tell his grandson. He hoped that somewhere, the boy heard them still.

After the man had sailed to nearly every corner of the world, climbed mountains, and crossed deserts, he stood on the deck of his boat one evening, staring up at the stars. And again, he heard one of them whisper in that familiar voice.

"Please come home."

The man knew then that he had finally sailed for long enough. It was time to take his stories and his sorrows back to the house by the sea. And so he did, though he was afraid of what waited for him there.

Then one night, not long after he arrived, he awoke to hear a noise in the empty house. He came downstairs to find a girl in his library. A girl who gazed up at him with wide, quiet eyes.

He understood then why his grandson had called to him.

And he was glad he had come home at last.

As Mr. Taylor finished his story, silent tears slid down my cheeks. Tears that had nothing to do with my burning elbow or throbbing knee.

"Batty was real" was the first thing I managed to croak out.

"What's that?" Mr. Taylor said. The whole time he was speaking, he had been staring out at the moonlight that shimmered on the ocean like the tail of a great silver kite. But now he turned to me.

"When I was little," I said, "I had this imaginary friend. Or at least I thought he was imaginary. Named Batty. He was going to be an astronaut when he grew up."

A shadow of a smile flitted across my grandfather's face. "You found your own way of remembering Matty, then."

"But my mom," I said, "she told me I shouldn't play with him anymore."

"Things weren't easy for your mother after Matty and Ben died," Mr. Taylor said, looking away again. "She and Ben were very close. That's what happens sometimes in a family where one member is absent. The others grow closer to make up for it. She and Clare never went anywhere without Ben. When Matty came along, he was like a son to her."

It was like there was a pocket in my heart that had been sewn shut all these years, and now it had been ripped open. Inside were the few memories of Matty I carried, and the love I must have held for him, and the sorrow of losing a cousin and an uncle I didn't even know I had. All of them were spilling into me at once.

They made me feel heavy. Too heavy.

Because I finally understood what I had seen in Mom's eyes that day she saw me playing with "Batty." Not shame. Not disappointment.

Pain.

Every time she looked at me, she must see Matty and Ben. She must see them being swept out to sea and sucked down, down, down.

All because of me, I thought, but I must have said it

aloud, because Mr. Taylor winced. "No, Miranda. You were just a child. A toddler. No one knew there was a riptide that day, least of all you."

I didn't know how to put into words how heavy I felt.

"Riptide?" I said instead.

"It's a very strong current," he explained, "that can suck even a strong swimmer like Ben out to sea. After it happened, I found out that they're very common around this island. Something to do with the way the current runs when the tide goes out of the bay. That's why I used most of the money I had saved to buy this place and had all the signs put up. If I could stop someone else from drowning, then at least Matty and Ben wouldn't have died in vain."

"So you didn't find the treasure?"

Mr. Taylor's brow furrowed. "Treasure?"

"Sammy and Caleb and I thought that was why you bought the island. We thought you found some treasure here ten years ago and then came back for the rest."

"My, you three have been busy, haven't you?" Mr. Taylor said. "And thorough, too. But no, if there was ever any treasure on this island, it's long gone, I expect."

"So why have you been coming out here?"

We both covered our ears as Safira let out another

deafening screech from somewhere behind us. Then Mr. Taylor pointed toward the lighthouse. "I told you, didn't I, that I promised to make sure that all the stories I collected would be remembered?"

"Yeah."

"I want to do something," he said, "to help Matty and Ben be remembered, too. Something to make this island a beacon of hope again, instead of a place of sorrow and fear."

"You're going to fix the lighthouse up?" I guessed.

"In a way. Do you know what an observatory is?"

"Isn't it a place where you go to see the stars? With telescopes and things?"

"That's exactly right," Mr. Taylor said. "There isn't one anywhere nearby. And the view of the sky out here, from the top of the lighthouse, it's incredible. That's why I wanted to take you and Matty up there to watch the stars that night." Little lines of sorrow dug into the skin between his eyebrows.

"So you're making the lighthouse into an observatory?"

Mr. Taylor nodded, casting his eyes skyward. "I always feel closest to them when I'm out under the stars."

"Like the woman in the story from Peru. The very last story you told us."

"Yes," he said. "The night after I heard that story

was the same night I heard Matty's voice telling me it was time to come home. Once I set sail, I got to thinking about how no matter what they believe, a great many people look to the stars when they need to feel less alone, or when they miss someone who's gone. So I decided I would build the observatory. I'll create a dome at the top of the lighthouse with telescopes and star charts. But in the keeper's cottage, and on the walls of the staircase, that's where I'll hang the stories and the objects that go with them. That way, I'll keep my promise. People will come and see them, and they will remember."

"Oh," I breathed. I could already see it in my head. The starlit lighthouse with stories lining its walls. It would be beautiful.

"I've been coming at night to make some initial notes about the views," Mr. Taylor said. "And to bring some supplies that I'll be needing for the renovation."

So that's what had been in the crates Mr. Taylor's neighbor had seen him hauling into his truck. Not leaving supplies. Building supplies. Putting-down-roots supplies.

For a long moment, we were quiet, each lost in our own thoughts.

Maybe Mr. Taylor doesn't blame you for Matty and Ben's deaths, hissed the voice in my head, *but Mom still does. And why wouldn't she?*

A whimper escaped my lips.

"Miranda?" Mr. Taylor said gently. "Are you all right?"

The pain in my arm was still bad, but there was a deeper pain in my chest, like I was being dragged down into the sea all over again.

"I know you think it's not my fault," I said. "And I know I was just a little kid. But if I hadn't gone after that starfish . . ."

"Do you remember the story I told you of the Bosnian refugee?" Mr. Taylor asked. "The one who convinced himself that he was responsible for his family's misfortunes?"

"Yeah," I said. "But the money he took had nothing to do with what happened to them. This is—"

"It's different and it's the same, too. Sometimes things just happen in life. Things that we can't control or predict."

"Then why do I feel so awful inside?" I asked, a sob slipping from deep in my throat.

Mr. Taylor let out a long, whistling sigh. "The man in the story made himself feel guilty because it was easier than feeling something else."

"But sometimes people *should* feel guilty," I protested. "Sometimes we deserve to."

"Sometimes," Mr. Taylor said. "Some guilt tells us we've done a rotten thing, and that we need to do what we can to make up for it. That kind of guilt comes from our conscience. But some guilt tells us that we're just plain rotten, and nothing we can do will ever change that. And that kind of guilt is a liar, Miranda. I would know. I spent many years with it before I learned not to listen. That I'll always have to live with my past, but I dont have to live every day *in* it."

I knew that kind of guilt, too. I heard its voice all the time.

Could Mr. Taylor really be right? Was it a liar?

The voice told me it was my fault that things between Mom and me were so broken. But it also told me that things might get better. If only I could just *be* better.

Now, though, I understood that when Mom looked at me, she saw Matty and Ben. She saw their absence. That was the burden she'd lived with all these years. There was nothing I could do to change that.

And if I couldn't fix it, nothing would get better between us.

I must have started to cry again, because Mr. Taylor was pulling me in to his chest, his shirt still sopping from the ocean. He held me gently and rocked side to side until my sobs slowed.

I sat up when Slug began licking the tears from my face with his hot tongue, forcing me to smile, just for a second.

"I'd better get you home," Mr. Taylor said. "Where

does Sammy's family think you are?"

I groaned. I hadn't thought of them since I had tried to text Sammy and Caleb. Surely Uncle Amar would be awake by now. Had he come up to check on me?

"They think I'm upstairs sleeping," I said. "Or they did."

"Oh dear," Mr. Taylor said, helping me up from the sand. "Let me just get Safira to come down."

He whistled between his teeth, and after a few seconds, the trees began to rustle again and an enormous shadow glided out. Even though I knew it was only Safira, I still shivered. Anyone would have been frightened to see that ghostly shape rushing toward them.

"Ladrão!" she chirped at me.

I stroked her head to show there were no hard feelings. "Hey, Mr. Taylor?"

There was one more thing I needed to ask before he took me back.

"Mmm?" He was fishing in his pockets for something to feed her.

"Why didn't you tell me who you were?" I asked.

He handed Safira a few nuts from his pocket and gazed down at me. "Your mother had her reasons for wanting you to forget everything here," he said. "Including me."

"But why?" I asked. "Why hide you?"

He shook his head. "You'll have to ask her that, Miranda. I wanted you to know the truth. I had hoped you might already know. But then you told me your grandparents had died, and that you had no aunts or uncles, and I saw that you didn't know. I decided it wasn't my secret to tell. I gave you a little push or two in the right direction, though, didn't I?"

I thought about this as we walked to the dock. "The sankofa story," I said. "You told me to look in the past like the boy in the story who went back to his father's town."

"I *advised* you," said Mr. Taylor. "But I left it up to you to decide. I didn't want to force you to uncover a secret you didn't want to find."

"What about the picture book?" I asked. "And the photo inside?"

He frowned. "What book?"

I suddenly remembered that I had folded the photograph into my back pocket. I snatched it out, worried that the water had ruined it. It was slightly soggy, but at least the image was still clear.

I handed it to Mr. Taylor. "I found it in a book you gave Caleb for the library. *Cecil the Starfish Gets Lost.* Did you give it to him on purpose?"

His eyes went wide when he saw it, and he shook his head. "No. I would never have given that book to the library. Caleb must have put it in the wrong stack.

It was always Matty's favorite. I even read it to you a time or two."

"I remember," I said. "I think—I think it's why I wanted to get to that starfish so bad."

"I see," Mr. Taylor said quietly.

"And I recognized Bluey in the photo," I said. "The dolphin. That's how I knew you were my grandfather."

"Ah, so you assumed the child was you?"

"It's not?"

He shook his head. "It's Matty. After the accident, I insisted you at least keep his stuffed dolphin. So you would have something of his."

"And you took the picture and the book to remember him by?"

"Yes." He hesitated. "But I remembered you, too, while I was gone, Miranda. All the time. And when you broke into my house that night, well, it was the best thing that's happened to me in many years."

"Me too," I said. "I'm really, really glad you're my grandfather."

He hugged me again, and I winced as he squeezed my elbow.

"Sorry," he said. "We need to get you to a doctor. Let's go."

But my elbow hurt, I thought, only because someone had pulled me from the water so fiercely. Because my grandfather had gripped me so tight to keep me safe. Because I was his family, and family was the most important thing of all.

Just then, a loud CRACK filled the air, and a red firework exploded in the sky. Slug must have seen it, or felt the vibration of it, because he yelped and skittered onto the boat, and Safira let out another earsplitting squawk. As we stepped aboard, fireworks from the festival thundered through the sky, unfurling in blazes of blue, red, green, and gold.

While Mr. Taylor started up the boat engine, I lay down at the prow and looked up at the fireworks bursting across the stars, feeling the hum of the motor and the rocking of the waves underneath me.

After everything I'd been through that night, I should have been more afraid of the water than ever. But I was so tired that my bones ached, and the waves actually started to feel nice, like I was in a giant cradle.

And there was something still tickling the corners of my brain. The words Mr. Taylor had heard whispered from the stars.

Please don't forget me.

Please come home.

Maybe it was just a coincidence. Him hearing the words I had carried in my heart for so long.

Or maybe the words I meant for Mom had been heard by someone else. Maybe Matty had carried them across land and sea until they had reached Mr. Taylor's little boat.

I stole one last look at the stars, and I thought that maybe I had never been quite as alone as I'd thought. Maybe wherever he was, Matty had never forgotten about me. Just like from now on I would always remember him and Uncle Ben. My heart would become their home, and they would stay there as long as I lived.

As the final round of fireworks floated down from the sky and my eyelids began to fall, I thought I glimpsed a star that winked down at me fondly. As if to say *Thank you.*

I don't remember sailing into the harbor that night, or the anxious crowd that waited for us there, including six policemen, two coast guards, and a hysterical Aunt Clare. Later, Uncle Amar would tell me that I didn't remember because I had been weak and probably in shock. I had only just made it down the dock, he said, before my knees gave out and I fainted.

Uncle Amar *had* gone to check on me upstairs, not long after I had left. When he called Aunt Clare and found out that I wasn't with them, Jai finally spilled the beans about our plans to go to Keeper's Island, and Sammy and Caleb came clean about everything. The police were just about to launch a search party when Caleb spotted Mr. Taylor's boat sailing toward the harbor.

But I wouldn't know any of that until later.

The next thing I knew, it was morning, and I was in a room that felt too bright even behind my closed eyelids. My toes searched for sand at the foot of the bed, but there was none. Everything felt too heavy— the sheets and blankets, my eyelids.

When I could finally open my eyes, I realized I was in a hospital room with cream walls and a picture of the ocean that was gray and lifeless, not at all like the painting above Mr. Taylor's mantel. A tube was sticking out of my left arm, and the sight of it made me cringe.

At first, I thought I was alone, but then I realized there was a sound coming from close by—breathing. When I managed to turn my neck, my heart leaped into my throat. A figure was slouched in the chair next to my bed, sleeping with a suit jacket draped over him.

"Dad?" I said. My voice came out all raspy.

His eyes fluttered open, and for a minute he didn't move. He just stared at me like I was some kind of work of art, studying every detail of my face.

"Hey, kiddo," he said finally, sitting up. His hair was rumpled, and a bit of drool was still stuck to his chin. He reached out and squeezed my right hand.

"What day is it?" I croaked.

"Tomorrow," he said. He fumbled to pour me a glass of water from a plastic pitcher and handed it to me. "Well, it's today, now, obviously. But you've only been here since last night."

"How did you get here?" I asked, once I had gulped down some water. It was easier to speak now. "What about your case?"

Dad waved the question away. "It's just a case. I got onto the first flight after Clare called to say they couldn't find you." He tried to force his lips into a smile, but his face just crumpled like a sandcastle collapsing in the tide. "I'm so sorry, Miranda."

"Why? What did you do?"

He shook his head. "I should have told you," he said. "You shouldn't have had to go looking for the truth all on your own. I wanted you to know. I didn't want you to come here without knowing, but your mom—"

He stopped, his face tightening.

"She's not here," I said, feeling the familiar blow of disappointment.

But then my eyes landed on two suitcases beside Dad's chair.

"Actually," said a voice from the doorway, "I am. It's a good thing I had already decided to cut my trip short. I was already on my way back when Clare called."

I whipped my head around. Mom stood there, holding a steaming paper cup in each hand. Her hands, I saw, were shaking. She was pale, her face pinched, her eyes cloaked in shadows.

I looked at her, but I didn't meet her gaze. I was too afraid of what I might see there. I stared instead at the green hospital blanket.

"I'm sorry," I said to the blanket. "I'm sorry I caused so much trouble."

Dad grabbed my hand again. "Miranda," he said, "you have nothing to apologize for. Nothing at all."

My shoulders began to shake. "Yes, I do," I said. "I know everything. About Matty and Ben. I know how they died." I chanced a glance at the doorway. "I know that's why it's so hard for you to be my mom."

Mom's face went even paler, and Dad blinked his eyes really hard.

"Leo?" Mom said. "Could I have a minute with Miranda? Alone?"

Dad looked at me, then at Mom. "Okay," he said. "I'll go let the nurses know you're awake. And everyone in the waiting room."

"Everyone?" I asked.

"The Grovers all insisted on staying," Dad said, brushing my hair back from my face. It still felt stiff with salt. "Your grandfather, too. And a boy—Carl?"

"Caleb," I said, feeling a little tingle in my toes. I

couldn't believe they had all stayed here overnight for me.

"You're going to be just fine, by the way," Dad said. "You had a dislocated elbow, and a cut on your knee that needed stitching, but the doctor fixed everything while you were asleep."

I moved my hurt arm and realized that it didn't actually hurt much at all anymore. Dad leaned over and kissed me on my head. When he got to the doorway, he took one of the cups from Mom's hand and murmured something in her ear. She closed her eyes and nodded.

When we were alone, she shut the door.

At first, she hovered there, like maybe she was thinking she should have left with Dad. Then she shuffled over to the bed and sat down beside my feet. The morning light etched little golden lines all over her face, so that she looked like a doll whose porcelain mask had begun to crack, finally revealing what lay underneath.

"You remind me a lot of your grandmother, you know," Mom said, tracing the rim of her coffee cup. "So loving. She was the one who was there for us when Taylor was working late or flying off on his next business trip. She was the one who taught me to love art. I wanted to be a painter like her when I grew up. I even went to school for it. I swore I would be like her, not like Taylor. But I ended up just like him."

I wasn't sure what I had expected her to say, but this was definitely not it. "You never told me about her," I whispered.

Mom took a deep breath. "When you love someone," she said, "it's like giving away a piece of your heart to them. And if something happens to that person, it's like that piece of your heart gets smashed to little bits."

"Is that why you didn't tell me about Matty?" I asked. "And Ben? And my grandfather?"

She ran her fingers through her knotted hair. "Partly. I'm not very good at being hurt, Miranda. Some people, when their heart gets broken, they try to pick up the pieces. They stitch them back together as best they can. But me—I just tried to sweep the pieces under the rug. Where they couldn't cut me up anymore."

She winced, and I wanted to throw back my covers and wrap my arms around her. But I made myself stay put.

"You said partly?" I asked.

"Partly it was to protect me from getting hurt. And partly it was to protect you."

"Me?" I could feel my eyebrows knitting together. "From what?"

Mom stared at the lifeless sea picture. "Like I said, you remind me of your grandmother. When you love someone, you love them with your whole heart. You don't hold back and you don't give up. That's how she was, too.

"Taylor said you remember what happened to Ben and Matty now, but after it happened, all you knew was that your uncle had pulled you from the water and that he and Matty had gone for a swim. You didn't understand. So when you asked me where they had gone, I told you they went on a trip. I didn't want you to blame yourself."

Tears welled in my eyes. Mom didn't want me to blame myself, but *she* blamed me.

"My heart was broken, worse than I ever thought it could be. Everyone's was. And I thought if I could just spare yours, maybe that would make us all feel a little better. Like not everything was broken. I thought maybe that's what Matty would want me to do."

"But didn't I want to know why they didn't come back?"

"At first, you asked every day," Mom said. "But then we left the Isle, and you only asked every other day. Then every week. Then eventually, they faded away, along with Taylor, the Isle, all of it."

"Except I didn't forget Matty," I said. "Not totally."

"No," she agreed. "A few months after you turned five, I came into the yard and saw you talking to someone who wasn't there. When I asked you who it was, you told me it was Batty."

"I always just thought I made him up," I said. "Like a regular imaginary friend."

"You didn't know you were remembering," Mom said. "I should have told you then. Your father begged me to tell you. But I just couldn't bring myself to do it. And the more time went on, the more impossible it seemed to do. And then suddenly ten years had gone by."

She took a small sip of coffee. Her hand was trembling.

"I remember how you looked at me that day," I said. "Like you were in pain."

A little smile tiptoed across her lips, but it didn't make her look any happier. "I told you," she said, "I'm not good at being hurt."

"That's why it's hard for you to be around me," I said quietly. "That's why you're always going away. I thought it was because I wasn't a good enough daughter. But it's because it hurts you to be with me, isn't it? Because you blame me."

Finally Mom turned and raised her fingers to my cheek, and I noticed for the first time how delicate they seemed. How fragile. They, too, seemed made of porcelain. When I met her eyes, they were swirling with shadows.

"No, sweetheart," she said, her voice firm now. "I'm sorry I ever let you think that. I don't blame you for anything. I wouldn't change you for the world. And it doesn't hurt me to be with you. The reason I—the reason I stay away is because I know how much you could hurt me."

The room went blurry as my tears spilled over. "I

would *never* do that," I sniffled.

"No," she said. "Not on purpose. But I was the one who got the call that night." Her voice became thick and shaky. "The call about Matty and Ben. I was with Matty's mom. We were shopping for Ben's birthday—that's why we weren't with you on the island. And I was the one who had to tell her that her husband and her son were gone, and hold her while she cried. It was the worst moment of my life. Then I came and sat in this very same hospital next to you, watching you while you slept. And I knew that if anything ever happened to you, I wouldn't be able to go on."

A sob escaped my lips. I hadn't even thought about Matty having a mother, but of course he would have. What had happened to her?

"After that, I started keeping you as close as I could. I barely let you out of my sight. Sometimes I even slept in your room, because if I didn't, I would just lie there, worrying about you."

"I remember," I mumbled. "But then you stopped. You went away."

"It started when you went to kindergarten," she said. "And I realized that I couldn't protect you every moment of every day. And if I couldn't protect you, I couldn't let myself be close to you. So I started working more. I gave up on painting and decided to try my hand at photography. I felt so much safer with the camera between me and the world. But it wasn't enough. I had to put something between me and *you*. So when I came home, I would try to pretend I was still gone. Then I would miss you and see I was hurting you, and I would try to make it up to you."

"Like our trip to Disneyland," I said.

She nodded. "Then I would get scared again and find another commission. I thought I was keeping my heart safe. But—"

Mom stopped, and her hand rose to her chest, which swelled in a sudden wave. "Then Clare called and said you were missing," she continued. I could see how every word was like a dagger twisting deeper in her chest, but I didn't tell her to stop.

"I had already decided after our talk the other day that I had to cut my trip short," Mom said. "I knew the second I heard you say Ben's name that I was going to have to tell you everything. When Clare called me in the airport, I felt this pain worse than anything I've ever known. All that time trying to protect myself from it, and I felt it anyway. And it was worse, because I knew if I lost you, I would never forgive myself for not being the kind of mother you deserved."

She bit her lip to stop it from trembling.

"I was wrong, Miranda," she said, her face screwed up with something like determination. "None of this is your fault. It's mine, and I'm sorry. I love you."

I didn't say anything for a long minute. The words "I forgive you" were waiting on the tip of my tongue, but for some reason, I couldn't say them.

"Will you say the last part again?" I asked.

"It's not your fault," Mom said. "I love you."

I closed my eyes and heard the words over and over again.

It's not your fault. I love you.

It's not your fault. I love you.

It's not your fault.

I love you.

I repeated them to myself until they were carved into my brain, like Mom's and Clare's and Ben's names carved into the sidewalk. Until I knew that I could go back and read them whenever I needed to remind myself.

"You talked to Mr. Taylor?" I asked. "I mean, my grandfather?"

"Yes," Mom replied. "He told me you've been getting to know each other."

"Don't be mad at him," I said. "*I* found *him*. And he didn't tell me who he was until I already knew."

Mom shook her head. "I'm not mad. At least, not about that."

"He's changed, Mom," I said. "He told me that what makes a family great is how they overcome their problems together."

"That sounds like good advice," she said.

"I guess—" I started. "What I mean is that I want *us* to be a great family."

"Me too," Mom whispered.

For so long, I had thought everything was my fault because I wasn't perfect. But Mom wasn't perfect either. And I realized then that maybe that's just what family was. People who loved each other even though they weren't perfect.

"Then I think I do forgive you," I said.

"Thank you," said Mom stiffly. Then she leaned down and planted a kiss in my hair like a seed.

Later that day, my doctor came in and examined me, then told me I could go home. Mom and Dad drove me back to the Grovers' house, where everyone else had finally returned that morning.

Sammy burst out the door and almost pounced on me before remembering my arm. She hugged me tight around my waist, squeezing a laugh out of me, before pulling away.

Caleb was behind her, and to my surprise, he hugged me, too. My stomach bobbed like I was still on the little sailboat as he wrapped his arms lightly over my shoulders. "You kind of had us worried," he said. "Pretty cool what you did, though. Guess this means I can't call you Sand Queen anymore, huh?"

I laughed again as he stepped away, then saw Aunt Clare standing by the door, her arms wrapped around Mom. When she turned around again and caught sight of me, her eyes were glistening, and my laughter fell away.

"I'm really sorry, Aunt Clare," I said. "I'm sorry we lied to you and Uncle Amar, and I'm sorry—"

"Miranda," she interrupted, her voice firm, "I accept your apology on one condition. No more apologizing, okay? I think you've done enough of that for a while."

"What about thanks?" I asked. "Can I say that? Because I'm really, really thankful for everything you've done for me this summer. I know you and Uncle Amar weren't sure about having me at first, but—"

"What do you mean?" Aunt Clare asked, cocking her head.

My cheeks flushed. "Well, um, I kind of overheard you guys talking," I said. "About how I was a burden."

Her eyes went wide as she looked from Mom and Dad to me. "Miranda, I would *never* say—" She stopped. "Oh," she breathed. "You mean the night after your first sailing lesson?"

I nodded.

"Miranda, the burden we were talking about wasn't you. It was having to hide the truth." She shot an apologetic glance at Mom. "We didn't like being dishonest with you, and when I saw that Taylor's ship had docked in the harbor that morning, I was worried it could complicate things. I should have called you, Beth."

"See?" Sammy whispered. "I told you they would never say that about you."

"I shouldn't have asked you to lie," Mom said. "It *was* a burden, and I'm sorry."

Then she and Aunt Clare embraced in another teary hug and disappeared inside, Dad trailing behind with his and Mom's suitcases. Sammy gestured for me to sit down in the hammock. Caleb took the rocking chair next to it.

"So. . . ," Sammy said, staring at me, "how are you?"

I could tell that, like a true journalist, she was bursting to know all the details of what had happened since I had last seen them. But, like a true friend, she wanted to make sure I was okay even more.

I told them everything. About the picture in the book, and the measurements on Mr. Taylor's wall. Their eyes went wide when I told them about sailing to Keeper's Island and Safira bursting from the trees, and they shook their heads as I told them Mr. Taylor's story, but they didn't seem all that surprised about any of it.

"You guys already know all this, don't you?" I asked.

"It was kind of a long night," Caleb said sheepishly. "There was lots of time to talk."

"Who told you everything?"

"Actually," Sammy said, "it was Jai who told us about Matty."

"*Jai?*" I asked. "Jai knew?"

"I guess he knew Matty before he, um, died," Sammy said.

"Oh." For the first time since yesterday, I felt a twinge of anger. Exactly how many people had helped Mom hide the truth from me all this time? "Are you in trouble with your parents?" I asked Sammy. "They aren't going to ground you from the newspaper, are they?"

"They're definitely grounding me," she said. "But only until the summer's over. And they're taking Jai's phone and computer for a week because he didn't tell them earlier about our plan."

"Sammy's mom called my parents, too," Caleb said.

My chin sank into my palms. "I'm so sorry, you guys."

Sammy shook her head. "Remember what Mom just said? No more apologizing. Besides, it was totally worth it."

"I think it actually made my parents realize that they haven't really been, you know, paying very much attention to me lately," Caleb said. "So you shouldn't feel bad."

The screen door creaked open, and Mom appeared.

"Kids?" she said uncertainly. "It's probably time to come in now and get ready."

"Ready?" I asked. "For what?"

"To go to Mr. Taylor's, of course," Sammy said. "Don't you remember? He promised us a party. Only it's a dinner party now, and there's going to be a lot more guests."

Even though Aunt Clare told me not to, I had to make one last apology.

Before we left for Mr. Taylor's—I knew I couldn't keep calling him that forever, but I still wasn't sure *what* I should call him—I slipped from Sammy's room. I stopped outside Jai's door, listening. I could hear him talking to someone inside, so Aunt Clare must not have confiscated his phone yet. I didn't really want to interrupt, but who knew if I would get another chance? So I knocked. The room went silent, and after a second, the door cracked open.

"Sorry," I said. "I know you're on the phone."

"No I wasn't," Jai replied, giving me a funny look.

"Who talks on the phone anymore?"

"But . . . we always hear you talking through the wall," I said. "We thought you were talking to one of your, um, girlfriends."

Jai rolled his eyes and opened the door wider. "I'm practicing."

He nodded to his desk, where a bunch of flash cards sat around an open comic book. There was writing on the cards in an alphabet I'd never see before.

"I want to go back to India next summer," he said. "But this time I want to be able to speak Punjabi. Fit in with my family and not feel like so much of a tourist, you know? I can almost read some of these comics now."

"That's really cool," I said. I didn't know what it felt like to need to learn another language so bad, but I *did* know what it was like to want to belong in your own family. "Why haven't you told anyone?"

He shrugged. "If I tell Dad, he'll get all excited about it. I guess I just wanted to make sure I could really do it before I told them."

"Told them what?"

We both turned to see Sammy and Caleb standing in the doorway.

"None of your business," said Jai at the same time as I said, "Jai's learning Punjabi."

"You *are*?" Sammy asked.

"Sure," he said. "It's a pretty cool language once you learn the basics."

"Dadi will be really happy," Sammy said. She hesitated, and then her eyes brightened. "Maybe we could, like, learn together? Dad would help us. We could have nights where we speak only Punjabi and stuff!"

Jai stared at her for a long second. Then he smiled. "Sure, little sis," he said. "We can work something out. But you'll be cleaning my room for a year."

She scowled, and Jai laughed. "I'm just kidding," he said. "Lighten up."

Sammy punched him in the shoulder.

"Anyway, what did you want, Miranda?" Jai asked.

"Just to say that I'm sorry for breaking my promise," I said. "I really wasn't planning to go to the island when I made it."

"It's okay," he said. "I probably would have done the same thing."

"Sammy said you knew Matty?"

"Yeah," he replied. "We were the same age. We used to play together sometimes. He knew the name for everything, you know? Dinosaurs, rocks, stars. I was really sad when he died. It's kind of the reason I became a lifeguard."

"Oh, wow," I breathed.

"But I didn't realize you were Matty's cousin. I was pretty young then, and the details are all fuzzy. I put it together after I heard you were looking for some-one named Ben. I remembered that was Matty's dad's name. And then I heard you talking about Keeper's Island, and I started figuring it out. I'm really sorry for, you know, everything."

At least Jai had only been lying to me for a couple of days. Somehow that made me feel a little better.

"Hey, Miranda?" he called, once I had turned to go.

"Yeah?"

"You remind me of him, you know. Matty. He always liked you. I bet he'd be proud to have you as his little cousin."

51

When we got to Mr. Taylor's house that evening, Mom hovered for a minute at the gates. Her eyes misted over as she stared up at the house, like she was under some kind of spell. Her fists clenched together like mine did when I was nervous.

Maybe we were more alike than I thought.

"It reminds you of them, huh?" I asked. "Grandma and Ben and Matty."

"It does," she said. "But that's okay. Not all reminders need to be bad ones, right?"

Just then, Betsy flung open the door and stepped out onto the porch.

"Beth!" Betsy cried, trotting down the stairs. She

was wearing a knee-length dress that poufed out at the bottom, and her hair was swept up in a knot. "Oh my, you're so—so beautiful! You look so different, but so much the same."

"Hi, Betsy," Mom said, as Betsy wrapped her in a hug.

"You guys know each other?" Caleb asked.

"I've been the housekeeper here for a long time," Betsy replied.

"That explains how Betsy's mom knew our moms," Sammy murmured.

Betsy went around hugging each of us until she reached me. As she pulled me close to her, careful not to crush my pie, she whispered in my ear. "I'm so sorry about the other day, Miranda. I wanted to tell you the truth, but Taylor swore me to secrecy."

"It's okay." I said. "I understand."

I suddenly remembered how once she had nearly pushed me out of the kitchen doorway. She'd said it was because the kitchen was messy, but it must have been because she didn't want me to see my and Matty's names on the wall.

"Come in, everyone, come in," she called, taking the pie from my hands. "Make yourselves at home. I'm going to take this pie back to the kitchen. I can't wait to taste it, Miranda! And I have something for you. It's in the kitchen. Just hold on while I—"

But her words faded when she zipped through the door. As the rest of us filed into the house, I heard a familiar squawking.

"Ladrão! Pega ladrão! Polícia!"

Beside me, Dad stiffened and tucked me protectively under his arm. "What's that?"

"It's just Mr. Taylor's parrot, Dad," I replied. "Relax."

"Parrot?" Mom echoed.

"She's a hyacinth macaw," Caleb said knowledgeably. "It's only, like, the biggest parrot in the world. Be careful of your fingers around her. She can break them like twigs if she gets them into her beak."

Caleb snapped an invisible twig over his knee, and Aunt Clare exchanged a look with Uncle Amar.

"Stop trying to scare them, Caleb," Sammy said, rolling her eyes.

We heard a creaking noise upstairs, and Mr. Taylor and Slug appeared on the landing. Mr. Taylor froze there a moment, just as Mom had done at the gates. His thin tuft of hair was slicked back, and he wore a button-down shirt and khaki shorts. Slug scrambled down the stairs, straight into Sammy's arms.

"Slug, meet everybody," she said. "Everybody, this is Slug."

But Slug was already flipped onto his back, eyes closing as Sammy stroked his belly.

Mr. Taylor made his way down the stairs as I pushed to the front of everybody. When he reached the bottom, I wrapped my arms around his back. I held so tightly with my good arm that he let out a small chuckle. "Quite the grip you've got," he said.

I took it as a compliment.

"You saved my life. I never said thank you."

"And you never need to," Mr. Taylor said, squeezing me back.

"What do I call you now?" I asked. "I can't keep calling you Mr. Taylor."

I didn't want to say it, because it felt mean, but "grandpa" didn't feel right either. Not yet.

"How about just plain old Taylor?" he said.

"Yeah," I agreed. "Taylor."

When I finally pulled away, his eyes fell on Mom. "Hullo, Beth," he said. His cheeks had gone pink as the inside of a seashell.

"Hi, Dad," she said, reaching out for a handshake just as he opened his arms for a hug. I realized it was the first time I had heard her call him "Dad."

"Oh," they both muttered. "Sorry."

Finally they settled on a one-armed embrace.

As she entered the living room, Mom gasped. "Mom's paintings are exactly where she left them," she said quietly.

"Grandma painted these?" I asked.

Mom held her finger out to the painting above the mantel and gently stroked the blue brush marks of the sea.

"She did," Taylor said. "And yes, I kept them just where she wanted them."

"They're really good," I said.

"She was a very talented woman," Mom replied.

"Do you think—" I started. "Do you think you could tell me about her sometime? I want to know more about her. About all of them."

I wanted to see pictures and hear stories about the time Grandma burned the turkey or Matty took his first steps.

Mom glanced at Taylor. "I think we can arrange that," she said. "But only if your grandfather agrees to help."

There was something else I wanted to know—what had happened to Matty's mother. My aunt. But I wasn't ready to ask just yet.

I really, really hoped she had found a way to be happy again, maybe with a new family. But I didn't know if I could handle it if I found out she hadn't. Because even if no one else blamed me for what had happened to Matty and Ben, I still heard the voice of guilt in my head when I thought about them drowning. The one that said: *It was all your fault.*

I was trying not to listen to it, like Taylor said. But

it was going to take me a while to learn to tune it out completely.

One day, I knew, I would be brave enough to ask about her. But I decided it was okay if that day wasn't today.

Betsy burst back through the kitchen door then, holding covered dishes in both hands as she swept into the dining room. When she returned, she dug her hand into the pocket of her apron.

"Ta-da!" she said, producing a yellow ribbon and handing it to me.

"What's this?" I asked.

Betsy clucked her teeth. "What do you think it is, silly? The judges said it was absolutely mouthwatering. They wanted the recipe for themselves."

I took the ribbon and gazed down at it. In shiny letters, it read:

105TH ANNUAL
August Isle Pie-Baking Competition
⟨THIRD PLACE⟩

"I won third place?" I asked.

"You won third place!" Sammy exclaimed, jumping up and down. "I forgot to tell you because of everything else."

"What did you win?" Mom asked, looking from

the ribbon to Betsy.

"The pie competition," Betsy said. "Didn't Miranda tell you she was entering? You must have done an excellent job teaching her to bake."

Mom shifted from one foot to the other. "No," she said. "Miranda did that all on her own."

"Aunt Clare helped me," I said, beaming at her.

Sammy's mom held her palms up. "You baked that pie all by yourself. That ribbon is yours and yours alone."

My fingers ran along each of its smooth tails. I had never won a ribbon for anything before. I was already thinking of where I could hang it in my room.

"Did you win first place?" I asked Betsy.

She shook her head. "Didn't get around to entering," she said. "As you saw, Mama's not been well. She wanted to come tonight, but I didn't think she was strong enough for it. She would have loved to see you two girls together, though. She would have liked to know that you were still friends."

Betsy was looking at Mom and Aunt Clare. Sammy and I glanced at each other. Betsy's mom *had* seen our moms together, in a way. Or at least she thought she had. She'd seen them in *us*. "Don't worry," Sammy said. "I think she knows."

The adults looked at her questioningly, but she went back to scratching Slug.

"I'm sorry about your mother, Betsy," Mom said.

Betsy nodded, her chin dimpling. "She's lived a full life," she said. "It's the natural way of things. Still, we always wish we had more time together, don't we?"

52

Everyone was starving by the time we all sat down
at the dining table. Betsy had made pork chops and
biscuits, something called fried okra, and something
called pimento cheese, as well as green beans and
applesauce.

For a while, people were too busy eating to talk
much, other than to ask someone to pass the biscuits.
Mostly we communicated in gazes and glances.

Every time she sat down, Betsy would notice an
empty spot on the table and suddenly announce that
she had forgotten something, or that we needed more
butter, or more sweet tea, and she would bounce back
into the kitchen.

A couple of times, I looked up at Dad sitting across from me, and I would catch him staring at me like he was afraid I might disappear. Next to me, Mom glanced around nervously every now and again.

Taylor, seated at the head of the table, kept asking how everyone's food was. His voice was oddly high, and he kept looking around like he was sure this was all a dream, one that he was bound to wake up from any moment.

"You should tell one of your stories, Mr. Taylor!" Sammy said finally.

"The one about the snow leopard," Caleb suggested.

"Or about the tulip," Sammy said.

"Stories?" Aunt Clare asked.

"Taylor collects them," I explained proudly, "from all around the world. He told them to us when we helped him unpack, and he's putting them all—"

I stopped short, looking at Taylor. I wasn't sure if he was ready to tell everyone else about his plans or not. He nodded.

"He's putting them in the lighthouse on Keeper's Island," I continued. "He's turning it into an observatory in honor of Matty and Uncle Ben."

"Is that true?" Mom asked.

"It is," Taylor said. "I bought the island after the accident. I think it's time someone did something with it."

"Matty would love it," Mom said. "And Ben, too."

From her voice, I was sure that Mom was crying, but when I looked at her, there were no tears welling in her eyes.

Maybe, I thought, there were tears you could see and tears you could only hear.

Maybe Mom had spent so long behind her camera and her doll's smile that she didn't know how to express some things like other people did. Maybe with Mom, I was always going to have to look a little more closely to know what she was feeling.

Taylor started to tell the story about the snow leopard. When he was done, Mom asked him when he'd been in the Himalayas. It turned out they'd been there only a few months apart. Then Jai asked if Taylor had ever been to India. When he said he had, Uncle Amar wanted to know everywhere he'd stayed, and eaten, and visited. Then Sammy went to the living room and retrieved several of the scrapbooks she'd filled with Taylor's pictures, and everyone passed them around the table, peppering him with even more questions about his travels.

When the conversation died down again, Betsy announced that it was time for my pie. She served each of us a slice with a little mountain of vanilla ice cream on top.

I watched Mom as she ate. She closed her eyes, and

for the first time since we got there, her face seemed to relax. "I can't believe you made this," she said when she had swallowed her first bite. "It's fantastic, Miranda."

"Best pie I've ever eaten," Dad said, digging in for another bite.

"Exactly what I've been saying," Uncle Amar said, winking at me.

I was glad that everyone liked it, but I wished they would slow down a little bit. I didn't want the night to end.

All of us around the table had taken different paths to get there. Some had had to go around the world and back again. But we had finally made it.

We were family.

We were together.

And we were home.

53

"*I can't believe you're* actually leaving tomorrow," Sammy said, sighing.

"Me either," Caleb agreed.

The three of us sat on the porch watching the very last sunset of my summer in August Isle while the grown-ups did dishes inside.

"I know," I replied. "It's gone by so fast."

A sea breeze combed over us, tickling our cheeks and rustling our hair. I didn't want tomorrow to come.

But the anchor of dread in my belly wasn't there anymore. At least, it wasn't so heavy.

"We'll talk all the time," Sammy assured me.

"You'll be back next summer, right?" Caleb asked.

"I hope I'll be back every summer," I said. "My mom and dad, too. We'll have to come for the opening of the observatory."

Taylor had told us over pie that he was going to try to have it ready for next summer.

"Which reminds me," I said, turning to Caleb. "Why didn't you tell us that Taylor was a first name when your dad looked up those property records? If I'd known his last name was Crawford then, I would have realized who he was."

Caleb shrugged. "I didn't know that Crawford was your mom's name," he replied. "And I wasn't there when you guys met him. I figured you knew it was his first name and he just wanted you to call him that. Like how I call my dentist Dr. Rick. I don't know . . . adults are weird about names."

"True," Sammy agreed.

"Yeah, I guess. Hey," I said, bumping Sammy's knee with my own. "I'm sorry there didn't end up being any treasures or criminals or anything on Keeper's Island. You didn't get your scoop."

A smile stretched over her face as she flicked her hair back. "What are you talking about?" she said. "A new observatory on Keeper's Island is probably the most exciting thing that's happened here for a hundred years. And I'm the only reporter in town who knows about it."

"You're right," I said. "And I'm sure Taylor will give an exclusive to Sammy Grover, journalist extraordinaire!"

"Actually," she replied slowly, "I've been thinking about that."

"About what?" Caleb asked.

"About my name. I want to be Sameera again, at least for my journalist name. I've been thinking about what Charlie said, about how if she were starting out as a scientist today, she wouldn't have changed her name. Because she was never ashamed of being a woman. It was just easier to get a job with a man's name."

"Who's Charlie?" Caleb asked.

Sammy ignored him. "And I'm not ashamed of being Indian, either. I never have been. I just thought it would be easier to fit in if I was . . . less Indian. But I'm proud of my family, and I want everyone to know it. So people are just going to have to get used to it. Because I'm not changing who I am for anybody anymore."

I slap her a high five. "And *I'm* really proud to have you as my friend, Sameera Grover. I wouldn't change you for the world."

"Suh-mee-rah," Caleb said carefully. "I like it. Just don't forget the little people, though. When you win your Academy Award or whatever."

"That's for movies, bonehead," Sammy said. "I'm going to win a Pulitzer."

"Either way, I get a mention in your acceptance speech, right?"

I giggled.

"Hey," Sammy said, "you never told us earlier what happened with your mom. Are you guys, like, okay?"

I took a deep breath and told them all about my conversation with Mom. I told them how when Dad came back to my hospital room, he said that all three of us were going to go see a counselor together when we got home. Someone who could help us learn to love each other in ways that didn't hurt.

"See?" Sammy said. "I told you it wasn't your fault. But I guess you needed to hear it from your mom, huh?"

"Yeah," I said. "I think I did."

"It's cool you guys are getting kind of a fresh start," Caleb said.

"What about you?" I asked. "Why didn't your parents come tonight?"

He kicked a pebble off the bottom step. "I thought about inviting them," he said, "but they can't be in the same room together. And I couldn't choose one and not the other, so . . ."

"What's going to happen now?" Sammy asked.

"I'm not really sure," he said. "I guess everything is gonna change."

"Not everything," I said quietly.

Caleb turned to me, eyes hopeful. "What do you mean?"

"Well, it's like Sammy said," I replied. "*You* don't have to change. I don't think we should let what's happening with our parents define us. Just because yours are, like, breaking up . . . it doesn't mean that *you're* broken."

"Yeah," Sammy agreed. "And you can come over to my house anytime you want."

The text message alert on Sammy's phone bleeped from inside the house, and she leaped up to get it.

After she'd disappeared inside, I cleared my throat. "I'm, um, here for you, Caleb," I said. "You know, if you ever need someone to talk to or anything."

The moonlight turned his cheeks silver. "Thanks, Miranda."

"Guess we should go back inside now, huh?"

"Guess so."

I stood up, but before I could go in, Caleb reached for my hand. My stomach suddenly went all sparkly inside.

"Hey, Miranda?"

"Yeah?"

"Um. It was pretty awesome what you did. Sailing

to that island all by yourself. You've kind of, like, made this whole summer awesome. I guess . . . what I'm trying to say is . . . I'm gonna miss you. Can I, um—?"

He leaned closer, and I felt my breath catch in my chest. I nodded.

With that, he leaned over and brushed a kiss against the corner of my mouth.

He pulled away just as Sammy barreled out from the house. "You guys!" she cried. "It's happening!"

"What's happening?" Caleb and I asked innocently.

Caleb cast a sheepish grin at me.

"The turtles," Sammy said. "They're coming up from the nest. We have to get down to the beach!"

"Oh, cool," Caleb said. "Let me just get my phone and stuff."

He disappeared into the house, and I raised my hand to my cheek. If not for the warmth I could still feel there, I would have thought I had imagined my very first kiss.

"What's up with you?" Sammy asked.

"Nothing," I said. I realized then that everyone had their secrets, but not all secrets had to be bad. Some things—a first kiss, an attempt to learn a new language—were okay to keep to yourself for a while. And besides, I would tell Sammy soon, just not right now. Maybe one day, I would even tell Mom. "This summer has been full of surprises, hasn't it?"

Sammy *herded all of* us from the house. Even Slug
helped, nudging up against people's knees as they filed
from the dining room back through the living room.
He stared woefully up as Taylor shut the door behind
Betsy, and Safira began to screech like I'd heard her
do on the island.

"That bird has one healthy set of lungs," Uncle Amar
said, covering his ears.

"Sounds kind of like you singing in the shower," Jai
replied.

"Just for that, I'm taking an extra long one tonight,"
Uncle Amar said, wrapping an arm over Jai's shoulders and ruffling his son's perfectly gelled hair. Jai

ducked away, scowling, while Sammy and I laughed.

"Do you think I have time to run back and get my camera?" Mom asked.

I bit my lip.

"Maybe not," Dad replied. "Maybe you can just be with us."

"Of course," Mom said quickly. "You're right."

Glancing around, I realized that Taylor had fallen behind. "You go ahead," I said to Mom and Dad.

I hung back until Taylor caught up with me.

"Hi," I said.

He smiled. "Hi yourself. How are you feeling?"

"Okay," I said. "My arm doesn't hurt anymore, and my knee's okay."

"That's good."

"How are you?" I asked. "How are things between you and Mom?"

"Put it this way," he said. "A month ago, I didn't think I would ever see her again. Or you, for that matter. The fact that I have both of you here with me—that's enough, for now. Don't forget, I put your mom through a lot, too."

"She'll forgive you," I said. "I know it. And then you'll come visit us and we'll come visit you. Maybe you can even come for Thanksgiving."

"I would like that very much."

"Hey, Taylor?" There was something I had been

wondering about since my talk with Mom this morning.

"Mmm?"

"Why do you think Mom sent me here?" I asked. "If she didn't want me to know about everything that happened?"

"I've been wondering that, too," he said. "It could be like you told me at the beginning of the summer. Maybe they just didn't have anywhere else to send you. They didn't know I would be here, and they probably thought one more girl would just blend in with all the tourists. There's not many of us left on the island who remember the accident now."

"Maybe," I said.

"Or," Taylor continued, "maybe your mom wanted to come home, but she didn't quite know how. Maybe she sent you to blaze a trail for her."

"What do you mean?"

"Well, I think the longer time went on, the harder it must have seemed to tell you the truth."

"Yeah," I replied. "That's what she said."

"So perhaps, deep down, part of her was hoping you would find it for yourself," he said. "Then she would have no choice but to look her past in the face. And then maybe she could finally come home again."

We walked in silence for a few seconds, listening to the laughter from the others carrying back and washing over us. "I feel like this is my home now, too," I said. "I wish I didn't have to go back tomorrow."

"This *is* your home," Taylor replied. "It always will be. I'll miss you when you go, but it's important for you to be with your mom and dad now. You three need some time together."

"Yeah," I said. "I guess. But what if . . . if Mom is just different right now because she thought I might be dead or something? What if things go back to the way they were before? I don't think I could take that."

Taylor swung an arm around my back. "I don't think that will happen, Miranda. Your mom told me she's not taking any more trips for the rest of the year."

"Really?" I asked, my voice squeaking with surprise. Hope floated my heart higher in my chest, like a buoy.

"Really," Taylor said. "But even if something happens and things go back to the way they were, you know who you are now, Miranda. Better than you did before, I think. No one can take that from you."

"But what if *I* go back to who I was before?" I asked. "The Isle has changed me so much. In a good way, I mean. I don't want to go back to being afraid all the time."

Taylor considered this for a few steps. "Sometimes," he said, "change is just discovering something that's been inside us all along. Take you, for example. Even before last night, I thought you were one of the bravest people I'd ever met."

"*Me?*"

"You."

"But *why?*"

"I think just about the bravest thing we can do is bare our true selves to the world, or to somebody, and ask them to love us. And that's exactly what you've done all these years with your mother. You never stopped loving her even though you've been hurt again and again. Lots of people, in that situation— they would guard their hearts. But not you, Miranda. Maybe you're too young yet to know how special that really is."

Taylor's words wrapped themselves around me like silk. Before this summer, nobody had *ever* called me brave. And now Taylor was telling me I'd been brave all along?

"Just look at your mother and me," he went on. "Both of us ran away to the farthest corners of the earth so no one could hurt us again. You're not like us in that way."

It *was* kind of strange how, even though they were apart, Mom and Taylor had chosen to live the same kind of life. "I guess Mom really is her father's daughter," I said.

"And you are your mother's daughter," Taylor replied.

"But it's up to you to decide what that means. Too many people in your life have defined themselves for too long by something that happened to them. Instead of creating our stories, we let our stories create us. Does that make sense?"

I thought about it as we climbed up onto the boardwalk and took off our shoes. "You mean what happened to Ben and Matty," I said. "You both let it take over your lives. And then you kind of . . . forgot to live them."

"Which is the exact opposite of what Ben and Matty would have wanted," Taylor said. "None of us can escape from the darkness in life, Miranda. But we can always choose to look for the stars."

We stood at the top of the boardwalk now, staring down at the moonlight glittering like confetti on the water.

"I don't want you to make the same mistakes as we did," Taylor said. "That's why I'm going to leave a space open in the observatory for your story. Whenever you're ready to tell it."

"*My* story?" I asked. "What's my story?"

"That's what I'm telling you, Miranda," Taylor said, pulling me in to his chest and kissing me lightly on the head. "It's up to you to decide. You and nobody else."

55

A small crowd of people was already on the beach, forming a line that reached from the nest to the sea.

"Oh, good!" Charlie said, catching sight of us. "You're here! Come look." She pointed down at the nest. "See how it's moving?"

It was hard to make out in the dark, but there was just enough moonlight to see that the sand had begun to bubble like a witch's cauldron.

"That's them climbing up to the surface," she said. "In a few minutes, they'll be starting down the beach toward the surf. You can all form a second line on the left there. Any turtles that get off course, just give them a very gentle nudge toward the ocean.

Otherwise, don't touch them, and keep quiet. Okay?"

All of us nodded, excited and solemn at the same time.

We formed a line across from the first one. Dad stayed closest to the nest, then Mom and me, then Taylor. Caleb stood on Taylor's other side, and the Grovers positioned themselves by the surf. Sammy leaned forward to give us a thumbs-up.

Soon we saw Charlie wave her hands.

"They're coming now," Dad said.

I craned my neck to get a better look. After a moment, tiny black specks appeared in the sand, slowly squirming toward us. As they neared, I could make out the shapes of their tiny flippers and heads.

"They're so small," Mom whispered. "They could fit in your pocket."

There was only a trickle at first, but then the beach began to fill with teensy turtles, crawling determinedly toward the silver sea. Mom and I both reached down as one began to veer off the path. We made a little wall with our palms. When the turtle bumped into us, it set off the other way, rejoining the line of its brothers and sisters.

We looked at each other and giggled.

"Matty would have liked this," I whispered. "Wouldn't he, Mom?"

She watched the turtle we'd helped as it inched

away, and a little smile made her cheeks bob. "He definitely would have," she murmured. "I guess we'll have
to soak it up for him, huh?"

Mom found my hand, laced her fingers through
mine, and squeezed.

Farther down the beach, we could just see the
shapes of the turtles as they made it to the water and
began to swim away, off into the ocean to start their
lives.

Mom and I stood together, holding hands until the
last few scrambled by. When they had all been swept
into the waves, a quiet cheer rose up on the beach.

"We did it!" I heard Sammy exclaim.

Dad walked around giving everyone high fives
while Taylor went to talk to Charlie. I let go of Mom's
hand and drifted away from everyone else, standing in
the surf where the turtles had just disappeared.

It was strange, I thought, how the sea had taken
Matty and Ben away, but tonight, it was giving all
these turtles a chance at a new life. It stung to know
that not all of them would have an easy time. Some of
them, like Matty, wouldn't even get to grow up. There
was no predicting where the tides would sweep them.

All they could do was keep swimming for the
horizon.

And one day, some of them would return to August
Isle, following in their mother's footsteps—or flipper

prints, that is. Just like I had. And the story would start again.

I thought about how I used to sit on my bed in Illinois, staring down at the postcards Aunt Clare had sent. How I had been looking for Mom in the postcards, but I had also been looking for *me*. I thought that if I could uncover Mom's past, I might discover the truth about myself.

But now I knew that the past might tell you *why* you were, but it couldn't tell you *who* you were.

Taylor was right. It was up to me to decide that. Matty and Ben's story would be in my heart forever, but it was finally time for me to write my own.

"Miranda!" Caleb was calling. "Come on!"

I turned to see him and Sammy standing by Jai's lifeguard tower. Sammy had unclipped a life jacket from it and was holding it in the air. "We're going swimming. Come with us!"

I looked back to where Mom, Dad, and Taylor stood with the Grovers.

"I don't know," Dad said, worry creeping into his brow. "It might not be the best idea."

"The current isn't very strong tonight," Jai said. "I'll keep an eye on them."

I met Mom's eyes, saw the surprise in them. She nodded. "If you want to go," she said, "it's okay with me."

"Thanks, Mom," I said. "I'll come back. I promise."

I skipped over to Sammy and Caleb, slipping my arms through the life jacket. "We're just going to go like this?" I asked. "At night? In all our clothes?"

"It's our last night together," Sammy said. "We should make the most of it, don't you think?"

"Yeah," I said, heart beating fast. "I do."

"I'll hold your hand," Caleb said.

"Me too," Sammy echoed. "We'll do it together."

"Okay," I said. "Together."

Then, with Sammy holding one hand and Caleb gripping the other tightly, I began to run. I waited to feel afraid. But the moon and the stars were shining down, illuminating the dark water, and I wasn't alone.

We collided with the surf and kept on running. And as I kicked off the sandy ocean floor and began to swim, the first words of my story suddenly appeared in my head.

I am Miranda, brave and bold, and I am my mother's daughter.

Acknowledgments

This story took me a long time to find. I am immensely grateful to those who stood by me while I searched for it, and to those who were there to help me bring it to life.

To Alyson Day, whom I count not only as an editor but a friend, for her patience, wisdom, and encouragement from the very start.

And to the rest of my truly wonderful team at Harper: Manny Blasco, Renée Cafiero, Janet Frick, Vaishali Nayak, Emma Meyer, and Aubrey Churchward for their loving care and attention to this book.

To Sarah Davies and Polly Nolan—literary agents extraordinaire—who have fielded more than their fair share of neurotic late-night emails, for never losing faith in me and for not letting me lose faith in myself.

To Sarah Coleman for lending her formidable artistic talents to the cover of this book, and Joel Tippie for the beautiful jacket design.

I had a lot of help telling Miranda's story. I am indebted to Tae Keller, Supriya Kelkar, Dusti Bowling, Kristin Gray, and Sally J. Pla for volunteering to be early readers of this manuscript, and for providing me with the insight I needed to craft it into the novel it has become. My thanks to them all for serving as teachers, friends, and inspirations to me along the way.

August Isle is a book of many stories, not just Miranda's, and I was fortunate enough to have support in writing those, too. I am deeply grateful to, among others, Devika Abrol, Emelia Asiedu, Devika Bhatia, Leah Henderson, Manayo Oddoye, Kristina Pugh, and particularly to Supriya Kelkar and Sangu Mandanna for lending me their time and wisdom to help me find and craft each story.

I could not have written this novel without all the friends and family who have rooted me on, listened to me fret, checked in on me, and told me they were proud of me along the way. There are too many to name all of you here, but please know that I feel extremely fortunate and grateful to have you all in my life.

To the Hatters, the UK 2017 debuts, and the 2017 middle grade debut group for all the advice, encouragement, solidarity, and laughs.

To Scott, Keith, Blakely, Paige, Emmalea, Taylor, Christie-Sue, and York for sitting around the table with me every other Thursday and gently shoving me in the direction of great(er)ness.

To Marilyn for teaching me that guilt is often a story we tell ourselves, and how to unwrite it.

To Molly, Becca, and Ingrid for always asking when they can read the next one.

To NRP for always reading every page of every draft and for saying, "I told you so."

To the Laaksos, whom I can always feel cheering me on even from across the ocean, for being my second family.

To Mom and Dad, who gave my story the best beginning I could hope for, and whose support means everything to me. Being able to share the good times with you makes the tough ones all worthwhile.

To Aki, who deserves more thanks than can fit in the pages of this book for his never-ending support these past few years, for being my inspiration, my rock, my shoulder, and my constant champion.

And to you, treasured reader, for coming on this journey with me. I hope you'll remember it as fondly as I will.

ALI STANDISH, author of the critically acclaimed *The Ethan I Was Before*, grew up splitting her time between North Carolina and several imaginary worlds. The only award she ever won in school was for messiest desk, but that didn't stop her from going on to get degrees from Pomona College, Hollins University, and the University of Cambridge. She still spends most of her time in her imagination, but you might just spot her walking her two rescue dogs with her Finnish husband around her neighborhood in Raleigh. You can visit her online at www.alistandish.com.

More books by
ALI STANDISH

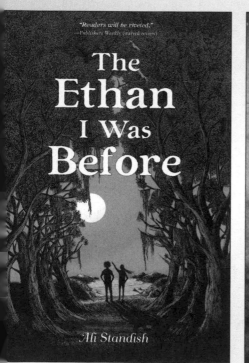

HARPER
An Imprint of HarperCollinsPublishers

www.harpercollinschildrens.com • www.shelfstuff.com